25 YEARS ON

Short Stories and Poems

HAMMOND
HOUSE

25 Years On
Short Stories and Poems

1st Edition published in the UK in 2019 by
Hammond House Publishing Ltd

ISBN: 978-1-9160980-6-0

Cover illustration by Adrian Sellers

Edited by Alex Thompson

Hammond House Publishing Ltd
University Centre Grimsby
DN34 5BQ, United Kingdom

www.hammondhousepublishing.com

Contents

Introduction

When I started Grimsby Writers twenty-five years ago, it was because there was a dearth of literary activities in the area. For a short period of time there had been WEA classes and a full programme of arts development led literary events. Carol Ann Duffy came to Grimsby to perform long before she became Poet Laureate; in fact, none of us had heard of her but we all went along and were inspired by her poetry. Then suddenly it all stopped. Local writers' felt deserted, bereft, abandoned.

I wrote to Trevor Millum, our WEA poetry tutor, telling him since his classes had ended, the writers of Grimsby no longer had poetry in their lives – could he help? He wrote back with the good news that he could get us funding for a series of writers' clinics – if I organised it. From the twelve people who enrolled in this programme – Grimsby Writers was formed.

Many people helped to keep it going and I would need the whole book to list them all. The growing numbers of writers who walked into Grimsby Central Library each brought their own contribution which enabled the group to establish and gain momentum. Some stayed while others came and went

– we had a saying once a Grimsby Writer, always a Grimsby Writer.

By joining forces with other writers' groups, we soon found ourselves performing outside of Grimsby. Networx was formed after I met Bill Allerton of Healey Writers at our NE Lincolnshire Literature Festival. It involved eight northern groups meeting once a month in Doncaster, sharing workshops and performing for each other.

As a result of this, Grimsby Writers became a member of the Federation of Worker Writers and Community Publishers (FWWCP – now The FED) which opened more doors and led to more funding.

Blocks of workshops with Trevor Millum, Mandy Sutter, Anne Rouse, not just one-off sessions, pushed us outside our comfort zones. However challenging this was members took it all on board. With increased confidence, members participated in local and seasonal events when invited by the council's Leisure and Library services. At one time it seemed Grimsby Writers were always in the Telegraph, which brought in more members.

A local writing group is essential support for writers in the area whatever their ambitions. Some people need help to get started, others need inspiration and motivation. It can sometimes be the first step to a career as an author.

Karen Maitland had her first novel produced as a direct result of coming to the writers' clinics that launched Grimsby

Writers. Karen was a member for several years and is now a well-known author of historical fiction with a unique mix of murder and magic.

Another member, Keith Gray, has also made a career as a successful writer and has won several awards with his novels for young adults.

I stood down as the chair of Grimsby Writers in 2001 in order to concentrate on my own development as a poet. I joined Driftnet Poets, the majority of whom were members of Grimsby Writers wanting to concentrate on writing and promoting poetry in the area. This they continued to do for over fifteen years through their performances and workshops across Lincolnshire and Yorkshire. Funded by Arts Council England, their most ambitious project Crossing Lines was a successful collaboration with visual artists and ended in an exhibition of poems, pictures and films at the Abbey Walk Gallery in November 2016. As a direct result of this several partnerships were formed, including my own with artist and poet Vivienne May. We launched our first book, Calling to the Moon, published by La Luna in May 2017. A book of pictures and poetry, all inspired by the moon, and represents the culmination of our creativity to date.

Last year Jackie Collins invited me to give a talk to current members about the origins of Grimsby Writers and a workshop on creative writing. It was a delight to see the group still flourishing and in such good hands. From my own experience, I know it takes hard work and dedication to keep a group thriving and developing. I wish Grimsby Writers every success with this book and all their future endeavours. I am honoured to be asked to write the introduction for this book.

As I write, the Words & Pictures Spring 2019 brochure has just come out. This follows on from a programme of exciting events and workshops in 2018 and continues the collaboration between La Luna and Lincs Inspire both having successfully secured further funding for our area. There has never been a better time to be a writer in NE Lincolnshire. It is a wonderful journey to be on – join in.

All good wishes and happy writing.

Maria Garner – December 2018

Feeling A Bit Rough
GRAHAM ALBECK

I've gone and caught a nasty cold
but I don't know where it's from?

It may have started when I got wet
walking down the prom.

A good thing to take for it is a lemon
with some honey,

But I would feel a damn sight better
if my nose wasn't quite so runny!

At least I can still taste my food,
and it's not as though I'm freezing.

So, I'll put some Olbas Oil up my nose
and try to stop this sneezing!

If it should keep me awake at night
I'll go and see a Nurse.

But it's not so serious, to see me
end up in a hearse!

'Keep taking the tablets!'

The Funeral
JOAN BARKER

The thunderstorm broke and heaven threw all available ammunition down on to the mourners as the cortege left the church. The deluge fell like stair rods on people and the already soaked churchyard. It was an ancient burial ground developed on sloping ground and the chosen gravesite was well away from the path.

The pallbearers stood to collect themselves and make ready for the forthcoming venture into rough territory, while the mourners adjusted clothing and raised their umbrellas in protest to the heavens. Steadily setting off in crocodile along the approach path to the site of the gaping hole, where it stood waiting to welcome the arrival of the new resident.

It so happened that the forward thinking of the undertaker had placed the largest pair of bearers at the front of the four. That seemed good thinking at the time but hadn't taken into consideration that the bigger the person usually means the larger the feet and more often than not, the clumsier the steerage. It also follows that the bigger they come the harder they fall.

The cortege neared the spot under the dripping trees that

preceded the trek across the sodden grass and slowly, oh, so slowly, the bearers carried their cargo down the slope to his new home. The gravediggers had completed their task in an earlier rain shower and dutifully placed green imitation grass around the edges, on the lines of wall-to-wall carpeting. However, helped by their meanderings back and forth, the grassy slope resembled a rugby pitch on winter Saturdays.

With everything to his disadvantage the leading pallbearer on the left couldn't be blamed for his right foot slipping on the mud at a critical point. Of course, four bearers are used with good reason and as a rule of thumb, one down means all down. As his foot slipped, so did his share of the load, setting in train an inevitable sequence of events.

There was only one place for the heavy coffin to go. Downwards. Into the expectant hole it began to slither. Credit due to the quick-thinking officiating vicar, his action was commendable if a little shocking. The congregated mourners and bystanders were treated to a spectacle to equal the best Brian Rix farce, giving them a morsel to chew on for weeks to come.

Placing a delaying priestly foot on the coffin as it bumped to the ground only accelerated its descent. He hadn't thought that even a vicar's shoe becomes slippery when wet and muddy. Although the remaining three bearers remained on their feet, the foremost bent to stop his colleague falling into the crater. His shoulder nudged the helpful cleric, whose foot slid the length of the polished coffin teetering on the edge of the hole, thus adding his considerable weight to the furthest end. This completely tipped the balance. The heavy wooden box completed its journey with the vicar sprawled inelegantly aboard, dragging the lowering ropes and the family wreath along for good measure.

All would have been well had the coffin slid into the desired position but it must have bumped the side of the grave wall which knocked off the lid. This element complete with vicar hit the bottom first, followed by the open coffin which landed upright. It was unfortunate for the mourners who had no wish to look on a dead Grandfather, for there he was, visible for all to see. Resplendent in his best black suit and black bowler hat. He looked very respectable and festive, with a red rose in his buttonhole and white handkerchief in his top pocket.

He would have been more impressive, had he not been standing on his head.

It was debatable whether the tears on the faces of the mourners were from hysterical laughter or grief, but, whatever the cause, there was pandemonium as the shocked and shaken vicar was hauled from his untimely experience.

After consuming two large medicinal brandies at the funeral tea, he was heard to say that he'd changed his mind about a burial for himself and was in favour of cremation.

Boudicca, A Bacon Butty And Me
DAVID BROMLEY

The Doctor had given me a thorough examination, and then he turned to me and said: 'I am sorry to tell you that you are going to die.'

'How long have I got?' I asked.

'Forty, maybe fifty years, perhaps even sixty if you are lucky.'

'What are you saying, doctor?'

'I mean, Henry, that there is absolutely nothing wrong with you, you are one of the healthiest individuals who has ever walked through my surgery door,' said the doctor.

'But the shooting pains in my head.'

'Pure imagination. The only thing you are suffering from is hypochondria so please stop wasting my time and for heaven's sake go out and get yourself a life. Time is precious, Henry, don't waste it, go out and enjoy yourself.'

I left the surgery, but I was not happy; the man might have more letters after his name than the average scrabble board, but he knew nothing. I had been a delicate child; Mother – and God bless her – always said so. If it was not my weak chest, it was my nervous stomach that kept me away from school for so many days when I was a child. I remember how often I would have to stay in bed and drink nothing but Bovril and have Mother rub petroleum jelly all over my chest.

I remember thinking I should report Doctor Ransaki to the General Medical Council. If he could not recognise a brain tumour when he saw one he ought to be struck off for incompetence. Once outside the surgery, I decided to go around to Gregory's the chemist. Mr Gregory could always find some medicine that would help, although it seemed to be getting more expensive all the time. Not that the price mattered, fortunately, Mother had left me well provided for after her death, so at least I did not have to worry on that score.

'Gregory's' is my favourite shop in the High Street: it smells so medicinal plus Mr Gregory in his immaculate white coat looks more like a doctor than most of the doctors do. In my experience, doctors can be a very scruffy lot, generally speaking.

'Good morning, Henry,' said Mr Gregory as I entered his shop, 'and what can we do for you today?'

'Shooting pains, 'I answer, 'in the head.'

'Ah yes, you must have watched that Panorama programme on brain tumours last night.'

'Yes, I did, it was jolly informative.'

'I am sure that I have something that can help, although I am afraid that it is not cheap. It is a special preparation that I make up myself, but the ingredients are getting so expensive these days.'

'That's all right if you think it will help me I will have it,' I said.

'Then I will go into the dispensary and make it up. If you need anything just shout.' This last remark addressed to a woman customer who was standing by Mr Gregory's selection of beauty products, but she did not answer.

I had not noticed her when I had gone into the shop, but now I could see she was quite a tall, well-built female. As she browsed the display, she had what I can only call a commanding presence. By no stretch of the imagination could she be considered beautiful but was unmistakably striking. Her long black hair flowed down her back and the firm, brave face reminded me of a picture of Boudicca that I had seen once at school. To be truthful, I am probably not the best judge of women, as I have not had very much to do with them. Mother always said that with my state of health it was best to avoid them, as it would only upset my chest or stomach.

I was looking at the shelf, which contained Mr Gregory's selection of cold and flu remedies, when the door banged open. A young man, no more than a teenager really, burst into the shop waving a kitchen knife. He had a wild, maniacal look in his eyes and vaguely pointed the knife in our direction as he went behind the counter. Firstly he opened the till and grabbed the notes, before turning to take some of the prescription drugs from the drawers behind the counter.

Without a word, the Amazon of a woman went behind the counter and took the youth by the collar and pulled him back. Once she was the right side of the counter the woman, who I could see dwarfed the teen, gave him a sharp blow with her elbow and the boy collapsed in a heap on the floor. She then smartly turned around, smiled at me and walked out of the door.

Just as she left Mr Gregory came out of the dispensary to find me standing over the unconscious unsuccessful thief. After that it all became something of a blur, Mr Gregory called the police who arrived a few minutes later. They knew the youth who they quickly hauled away to the police station. The pharmacist kept talking about my bravery and how I deserved a medal but for what I was not sure. Then two men from the local paper turned up, and one was a photographer who took Mr Gregory's photograph and then mine. The other, a reporter, asked a few questions which the chemist mainly answered because I did not know what to say. Neither of us mentioned the woman who I had by now named, in my mind, Boudicca.

Because of all the excitement, it was almost lunchtime when I left the shop, and it was not until I reached home that I realised I had forgotten to pick up the medicine Mr Gregory had made up for me. Not that it mattered as the shooting pains had stopped and I was feeling surprisingly well considering the morning's traumatic events. As I walked down my street, I bumped into old Mr Taylor, a neighbour, who also suffered poor health and we would often stop for a chat and to exchange symptoms. Today though, he could not linger, as he needed to get home, because he was having problems with his colostomy bag. It was a pity really because I would like to have told him about my morning's adventure.

Despite feeling much improved I decided that after all the commotion the best thing I could do after lunch was to go to bed. It is a known fact that too much excitement can raise the blood pressure and we all know what can be the result of this. During the afternoon I read some of my back copies of The Train Spotters Journal, but somehow I could not concentrate. I think the incident in the chemists had upset me more than I had initially thought. I stayed in bed until teatime when I decided to take a walk into town to the late-night pharmacy. Although the shooting pains had disappeared my stomach had started to play up and I was surprised to discover that I had no antacid tablets in the house.

Usually, I am the kind of person people ignore, which suits me fine, but that day as I walked towards the town people nodded and smiled at me. Some of the passers-by who I did not even know said, 'Well done, Henry,' it was all very confusing. However, it all became clear when I turned into the Market Square, and a youngster who could not have been more than ten rushed up to me and stared into my face.

'Look, Mum,' said the boy turning to a woman, presumably his Mother, 'It's Henry the Hero.'

'Oh, so it is,' the woman replied, 'but don't point Elvis, it's rude.'

Then turning to me she said, 'I am sorry, but he has never seen a live hero before. Would you mind autographing my copy of the evening paper, because to tell the truth I have never met a real hero before either?'

I looked at the newspaper she thrust towards me, and I was surprised to see my face staring back from the front page. It was the one taken in Mr Gregory's that morning and above it was the headline in large type, 'Henry the Hero.' To say I was surprised would be an understatement and I signed my name on her newspaper in a kind of daze. Me a hero, what nonsense but even so I felt a surge of pride, even if it was undeserved.

I had another surprise at the late night pharmacy when the chemist gave me two packets of antacid tablets but would not accept any payment.

Handing me the packets he said, 'What you did for a fellow chemist was above praise. I would not dream of taking your money.'

Walking home I had some feeling of guilt for all the unwarranted praise, but on the other hand, it was possibly the first time in my life that anyone had ever taken real notice of me and I liked it. So I was in quite a jolly mood when I turned into my street, and that was when I smelt the smoke. At first, I could not see where it was coming from although it soon became apparent it was streaming from the upper windows of number forty-seven. There was no doubt about it, the house was on fire, and somebody should do something about it, but what? I was standing in front of the house thinking about this when I heard a child crying, and the sound appeared to be coming from one of the upstairs windows.

As you may have deduced, I am not exactly the quickest of thinkers, but eventually, I reached the decision that somebody definitely should do something. However, I had not come up with any idea what that should be, when Boudicca, the woman from the chemists, rushed past me and went into the house. 'Call the fire brigade,' she shouted as she disappeared into the building. I think she yelled that but, it might just have been a voice inside my head, I am not sure. Of course, that is what I should have done in the first place and getting out my mobile I punched in three nines.

Boudicca seemed to be in the house for a long time, and I was beginning to fear that both she and the child had perished. However, eventually, she appeared through a cloud of smoke holding the now unconscious child in her arms like a trophy of war. I could also hear the sound of sirens in the distance that heralded the arrival of the emergency services. Boudicca ran across the front garden and handed the child to me; it was no more than a baby really, and I took it in my arms.

The child's parents and the fire brigade arrived at the same time, and it all became very chaotic. The mother took her baby from me, and the father grasped and hugged me, not a pleasant experience, and thanked me profusely. I turned to look for Boudicca, but she was gone. Soon afterwards an ambulance arrived and swept mother and baby, a girl, off to the local hospital. Last to appear was the police, by which time the fire was under control, and a large crowd had gathered to view the incident. I thought that this was a good time for me to leave and go home but I was stopped by a young police officer who told me I needed to make a statement which I did but making no mention of Boudicca or the rescue of the little girl. I merely said that I had seen the smoke and called the fire brigade, which was true.

Again, I was just about to leave when the same young reporter I had met that morning arrived and started asking me questions. I could not help him very much, and I was pleased to note that this time there was no photographer. Eventually, he went across to some of the spectators to get their stories, and I was able to slip away pretty much unnoticed. Once home I made myself a cup of Horlicks and had my usual digestive biscuit and went to bed. As I undressed, I found the two packets of antacid tablets, but again I realised that despite all the excitement of the previous hours my stomach had calmed down, and I felt better than I had done for a long time. Perhaps had I known what lay ahead the next day, it would not have been so calm, but in ignorance, I slept the sleep of the just.

The next morning a loud knocking on the front door woke me. Putting on my dressing gown, I went downstairs to see who on earth would be calling that early in the morning. When I opened the door, there was as a sea of faces looking at me and thrusting cameras and microphones in my face.

'How does it feel to be a two times hero?' one of the faces shouted at me. Another started to ask, 'Were you not afraid...' But the phone began to ring and so I said, 'I am sorry, but I have to answer the phone,' and closed the door on them all.

The phone call was from the Daily Trumpet and someone calling himself the News Editor who wanted to know if they could buy my story.

He seemed quite put out when I told him I did not have a story and put the phone down on him. After that, the phone never stopped ringing until I pulled out the plug on the wall. The crowd outside the front door seemed in no rush to disperse, and I did think about calling the police to ask them to move them on, but that would have meant connecting the phone again. My mobile's battery was flat when I tried to use it although on the screen a message appeared saying I could make emergency calls, but I was not sure this constituted an emergency.

Usually, I would be quite happy to stay in the house, but with the continual knocking on the door and the peering in at the windows I felt like a goldfish in a bowl and had to get out. People were turning my quiet world upside down, and I did not like it. I needed to escape. I went back upstairs and dressed before carefully opening the back door. I was thankful to see that it appeared clear so grabbing my train spotter's notebook I slipped out. The back gate leads into a passageway, and that too was free of reporters, and I was able to walk away without being seen.

There is nothing. I used to find more relaxing than sitting above an embankment watching the trains go past. Of course, it is not like the good old days of steam, with The Flying Scotsman, The Mallard and the other Pacific Class locomotives regularly passing through our station, but even the diesel and the electrics have a charm of their own. One of my favourite spots is the railway bridge that goes over the river just on the outskirts of the town. Usually, I would take some sandwiches and a flask of tea because Mother had drummed it into me never to use local cafes. She said you knew how unhygienic they were and with my delicate stomach, I had to be careful. However, in my rush to escape from the house, I had forgotten to bring anything to eat, and as I had had no breakfast, I was beginning to feel hungry. There was a small café near the bridge, so I decided to risk it. Surely there could be no risk of Salmonella in a packet of crisps and a bar of chocolate.

I was quite surprised how clean it was inside the café nothing like the vision of a hells kitchen that Mother had painted. As I opened the café door, I was met by the most wonderful smell of frying bacon, which I now think is the most seductive smell in the world. I just stood there inhaling the aroma and listening to the sound of the sizzling bacon in the pan. All at once all thoughts of chocolate or crisps fled from my mind. We had never had fried food at home, 'far too unhealthy' Mother had said, but oh the smell of fried bacon was irresistible.

'A bacon sandwich, please,' I said on impulse to the man behind the counter.

'Right you are, one bacon butty, coming up,' he answered, and within two minutes I was biting into the most delicious sandwich I had ever tasted. Sitting at a table, eating my bacon butty, with grease running down my chin I felt as though I was in food heaven. As I walked back to my spot by the bridge I could not believe I had lived so long without discovering the delights of the bacon butty. If I did subsequently go down with Botulism or Salmonella, then it would have been worth it just for the wonderful taste and smell.

The river was only about fifty yards across, but the railway bridge carried on over a road that ran parallel to the river. The best place to spot the trains was on a bank just above the street where you were almost level with the bridge. If there were not many trains, you could also watch the passing road traffic from there as well.

I had been sitting for about an hour, relieved that I had not succumbed to food poisoning, and was contemplating a second visit to the café when it happened. A little red open-topped sports car was coming along the road beside the river when it suddenly veered off, hit the railings separating the street from the river and somersaulted into the water.

It was instinct I suppose that made me run down towards the river, and by the time I got there, a small crowd had gathered looking into the water. However, no one seemed to be doing anything, but I was not worried I was sure that at any moment Boudicca would make an appearance and come to the rescue. I looked around but there was no sign of her, where the hell was the woman, I thought when you wanted her? After my experiences of the previous day, I was sure she would appear, but she didn't.

Somebody had to do something, and before I knew it, some fool had taken off his jacket and shoes and dived into the cold water. The most surprising thing was that I was that fool. Fortunately, I had learnt to swim at school but as soon as Mother found out that we had our lessons in a public pool she had written to the school telling them I was not to go there anymore because of my delicate condition.

When I saw the car disappear into the water I was pretty sure there was only the one person in the car. I kept diving down trying to see any sign of the driver or the vehicle. The riverbed was very muddy, and it was difficult to see any distance, but I had to try. I had just started wondering what Mother would have thought about me swimming in the dirty river when I spotted the driver, still trapped in the car. The driver, a girl, was still held in by her seatbelt and appeared to be unconscious. The first problem was to release the seatbelt, and not being a driver myself I was not too sure how they worked, but by trial and error I found the release mechanism and started to haul the girl clear of the car.

I cannot claim to have any life-saving skills or training, I just grabbed the collar of her jacket and pulled her behind me until we hit the surface. Then I made for the shore where willing hands helped to pull us ashore. As I lay on the bank trying to get my breath back, I could hear the sound of sirens approaching. They were becoming a pretty familiar sound these days. I knew what I had to do, and while everyone's attention was on the young driver, who appeared to be regaining consciousness, I got up and slipped away through the throng of spectators. As I walked away, I thought I saw Boudicca standing on the edge of the crowd and she was smiling at me, embarrassed I turned away for a second, but then when I looked back again she was gone.

All of that happened six months ago. Of course, inevitably I was recognised by someone at the riverside, and before long the press came back knocking on my door and to be honest I started quite to enjoy the attention. I even went on to the breakfast television news programme, and that was very interesting. I also had to go to the Town hall to be presented with a special award from the Mayor. After all of this fuss, I wanted to get away for a break, and that was when I saw an advertisement for a holiday in the USA. It involved something called White Water Rafting, although I did not know, at the time, what that was it did sound exciting. It was on this holiday that

I met Simone who it turned out only lived a few miles away from me back in England.

Since we came back from that holiday, I have seen quite a bit of Simone. We have a great deal in common, and we both love bacon butties. Next week we are going away together to Tanzania to do a sponsored climb of Mount Kilimanjaro. I have only seen Doctor Ransaki once in the last six months, and that was to get a Yellow Fever jab for this upcoming holiday. He seemed quite pleased to see me when I went into his surgery.

'How are you, Henry?' he asked

'To tell you the truth Doc, I don't think I have ever felt better.'

'And I don't think I have ever seen you looking fitter,' he said as he pushed the needle into my arm.

Looking back there was just one thing that I regretted, during the confusion at the riverside I lost my train spotters notebook. In it was a list of all the trains that I had spotted from the age of eight. To be entirely truthful, I am not that bothered as I have a feeling that I will never go trainspotting again; somehow it seems to have lost its fascination. As Doctor Ransaki said, time is precious and far too valuable to waste, and so now I have stopped just watching trains or for that matter life go by; now it is time to stop watching and jump aboard to see where it is going to take me.

Me Mam
BRENDA COLE

Give me a title I said to this man
OK bread butter and jam.
It was there in a flash it was me Mam
Bottles and bottles of jam she made
We stored in a cupboard like a big cage
We had gooseberry strawberry cranberry raspberry
Apples plums rhubarb and blackberry
On picking this fruit it seemed so endless
but products she made they were priceless

The smell that came flooding out of the fruit
When boiled up with the sugar it rose in the pan
This is how I remember me Mam

She'd stand in the kitchen all day long
Never a bother always a song
We all had a turn to see if it was set
out in a saucer previously wet
You just let it cool and put in a finger
The taste of it sticking to palette to linger

If its set you see it kind of wrinkles
But you always hoped it wasn't just right
as we'd run out of turns and us kids had a fight
She stirred it round with a big wooden spoon
which we also licked if she left the room

We had drinks of it to get rid of a cold
It's a country remedy to I'm told
We had jam tarts and dumplings too
I've even used as a kind of glue.
We also had doughnuts all kinds of cakes
The air perfumed from the oven when baked

While cooking the jam on top on the ring
She'd use the oven for bread cakes and sing
Come Sunday tea time
we were in for a treat
I never bothered not having meat
I always had hot bread butter and jam
made for me
by my Mam

Flesh & Blood
JACQUELINE COLLINS

Father David worked in the small vicarage garden. It was late autumn; the bright red and soft pink geraniums were still in flower; the night stocks filled the evening air with their sweet fragrance. He deadheaded the last few marigolds and pansies, meticulously collecting the flower heads, to dry out and replant the seeds in spring. Moving to the vegetable patch he weeded and watered, it had supplied salad items and vegetables that you could not buy in the shops due to rationing. He filled the large steel watering can from the outside tap and sprinkled a handful of blood fish and bone into the water, he emptied it along the row of bramley apple trees, thinking to himself, 'God only knows how Farmer Shepherd got his hands on extra blood, fish and bone.' David wasn't asking God or the Farmer. Father David tended his garden as lovingly and gently as he tended his flock, trying to provide what was needed to nurture. His garden was a source of escape and contentment to him during these troubled times. He lost himself for hours in digging and planting.

His thoughts and feelings were diverse this evening. The war over; the whole country just waiting for a final announcement. This meant that David's only son Phillip would be coming home. Pip, like all the other young men in the village of Buckden Oak had answered Lord Kitchener's call, 'Your Country Needs You' and had joined the Buckden Oak Pals. After a few weeks of basic training the boys were dispatched to France. Father David cast his mind back over the many hours he had spent consoling parents whose sons had been killed, or young wives whose husbands had returned minus a leg or an arm, blind or deaf. Each time he comforted such a family he selfishly prayed that Pip would not be next. 'Thank God,' Pip had been spared and that was cause for celebration. Father David recalled the book of Genesis, the exact words escaped him, but it was something like, 'Each war contains the seeds of a fresh war.' Pip was returning to a conflict that as yet he was unaware of. As Father David looked up at the attic window Sally passed it, cradling Charlie in her arms.

Sally looked down on the crying child. Her Mother had once told her that a baby knows if it's not wanted. Well, she never wanted Charlie, in fact she tried everything she knew to 'get rid' of him, gin, hot baths and potions purchased from back street abortionists. None of it worked and then she was 'too far gone' to try anything else. She sat in the wicker nursing chair by the attic fireplace and offered Charlie her breast. Thankfully he drank and settled.

Closing her eyes, she reflected on her seventeen years. As a child she lived in vastly overcrowded tenement buildings.

Her Mother took in washing, mending and cleaned other people's houses in order to pay the rent and feed her eight children. She was constantly tired. Her Father drank. At the age of 30, whilst working on the West India Quay, unloading a sugar boat, he got hit by the heavy tackle and was crippled from the waist down. Some said he had been drunk, but he denied it. Sally was used to being cold, hungry, and having no shoes on her feet as were most of the children around her in Limehouse.

At the age of fourteen Sally blossomed into a beautiful young woman. She had violet eyes and long straight black hair that shone, her skin was clear and olive coloured, she was slim and tall and had an air of confidence that made her seem older than her years. Sally started to turn heads, male heads, she began using her charms on the boys in her neighbourhood, they would give her things apples, a penny or do things for her if she smiled at them nicely and flirted a bit. Sally soon realised that older men were looking at her, they had more to give then the boys, but they wanted more for it.

Sally's Mother was worried about her daughter. Through acquaintances at Church she found Sally a position as kitchen maid, with a 'Christian family', as she put it, in St James Square. Mother said 'It would be hard work, but the opportunity was there to improve yourself.'

Sally did not much like being a servant. She found the hierarchy of the downstairs quarters equal to that of those upstairs and as kitchen maid she was about as low down the chain as you could get. She was well fed, warmly clothed and her slim figure filled out and took on curves in all the right places. Sally was now a rare beauty.

There were six girls in her tiny bedroom, four of them in one bed, she and Eliza topped and tailed with Jane and Lucy. Eliza had been working at the house for 3 years and she didn't enjoy 'waiting on' any more than Sally did. As they lay in bed at night, Eliza would tell Sally of her cousin, who worked in the centre of London and always had the latest fashion outfits, leather shoes, jewellery, make-up and time of her own to do as she pleased with. Her cousin said 'there were always jobs for pretty girls, if you were willing'. Eliza reckoned that a few hours on your back had to be easier than fourteen hours on your feet each day.

By the time Sally was sixteen she and Eliza had run away from St James Square. They worked from a dilapidated old house. The damp, plastered walls had once been painted with distemper in blue and yellow. The colour had faded, the plaster was falling off. There were large black circles of mould growing on the ceilings. In the yard there was one tap and one toilet, which served 12 houses, including the brothel. The girls seldom brought clients to the house. They were tolerated, accepted as a necessity, but not liked by the families in the street. Madame Louise oversaw the house; Madame was a hard woman, but by all accounts, better than a pimp. She took care of her girls, making sure they were not beaten up or badly treated.

They picked up lonely soldiers and sailors, on leave, who could provide cigarettes and alcohol, sometimes, stockings or lipstick. Wealthy older men, brought theatre tickets, meals in expensive restaurants and rented plush hotel rooms for the night. The girls always charged an escort fee.

When Sally realised, she was pregnant, she returned to her Mother, who was disgusted with her and turned her out. Pregnancy outside of marriage was a sin and a huge disgrace. If Sally had known who the Father was her Mother would have forced him to marry her. No home, no money, Sally desperately tried to think of someone who might help her.

The germ of an idea formed in Sally's mind. She remembered her Mothers second cousin Aunty Gina, everyone referred to Gina as 'Ma'. 'Ma' was married to a vicar; Father David had been the bain of Sally's formative years. Whenever she did anything wrong, (which was often) she would be revered with 'Whatever would Father David say!?' She had a distant memory of having met this family when she was small. She knew they lived in a little village called Buckden Oak, on the South Coast and that their standard of living was better than her own families. Sally remembered they had a son late in life. Pip, he would be 22 now and undoubtedly at war.

Sally arrived at the vicarage door, on a dark, cold, February evening. As 'Ma' opened the door, Sally broke down in tears and quickly blurted out her lies. She told how she met

Pip whilst he was on leave in London a few month ago Pip had desperately wanted to get home to see his parents, but the trains were not running and he only had a few days. They met purely by accident in St James Park; she was working as a kitchen maid nearby. They had a romance, which had resulted in her being pregnant with his child. Pip had talked about taking her home to meet his parents in Buckden Oak and of marriage. She was certain when he returned from the war, he would marry her. She had not written him of her pregnancy as she felt he had enough to contend with in France. She begged and pleaded with them to take her in, and not to write to her Mother, until she was a respectable married woman.

Father David felt obliged to help this fallen woman and doubly obliged if his son was responsible. The much-respected Vicar of Buckden Oak, had taken a lot of criticism from his flock over this situation. He had continued to carry out his duties as usual and tried to ignore the remarks and looks that came his way. He put his trust in God, and waited for all to resolve itself as things always did in the end, for good or bad.

Ma had her doubts about Sally's story. She was certainly pretty enough to turn any man's head. Ma had seen men in the village look at her. Although, Sally appeared a sweet, young, innocent girl, so grateful and helpful. Ma felt something was not quite right. Three months ago, Charlie had been born, Ma could see no resemblance to Pip, he was dark like his Mother.

Sally laid Charlie in the little slatted pinewood cot. She'd had a good nine months. Ma and Father David had looked after her and Charlie, but now, Pip was on his way home and would of course deny the whole thing. She packed her few belongings; tomorrow she would board the early train to London while everyone in the vicarage was still asleep. She didn't really care what would become of Charlie; she knew Ma and Father David were fond of him and hopefully would not abandon him, even when the truth came out. She looked in the large wood surround mirror that hung over the flowery porcelain bowl and jug, smiled her brightest smile, piled her raven hair up on top of her head and let ringlets drop around her face, she pinched her cheeks until they were rosy. She still had youth and her looks, she would return to the life of prostitution, a little older and a lot wiser.

The Night Brigade
MIKE COLLINS

The Ladies of the lamp go swiftly by.
In the dark of the night their skills to apply.
To a new arrival in all his plight.
1, 2, 3 lift, then tuck him in tight.

Cannulas on the left, cannulas on the right.
To no avail they search all night,
Needing a vein, his throb to rein.
Then with a flush the doctor came.

Giving spray of mist and puff of air,
All help to keep the air ways clear.
Onward, with mask, drip and pills.
Kind hands move fast to cure all ills

Fill the jug, empty the drain,
All to ease the patient's pain.
From bed to bed throughout the night,
Forward, no waver till morning light.

Tired and weary their duty done.
End of shift has finally come.
Honour the oath they made.
Honour 'The Night Brigade'.

A Perfect Match
MARIA GARNER

Louise put down the phone and sighed. Some days she hated this job. The Call Centre was not that bad, just not what she had imagined she would be doing when she left school.

'Hello. My name is Louise. I'm representing…' Here we go again. 'No, I'm not selling anything. I'd just like to ask you a few questions. It will only take five minutes of your time and you could win a…' The line went dead.

Louise sighed. How was she supposed to ask fifty questions if they hung up before she had even started? It was eleven o'clock and she'd only completed three questionnaires. One of those she'd made up half the answers. The bloke asked her more questions than she asked him. Finally, in frustration, she had put the phone down on him.

This week she was on CS - Cold Start. She loathed it. Fortunately it was only one week in four. When she thought about it, which was often these days, there was not much about the job she did like. Why did she stay? There was only one reason. She watched him out of the corner of her eye. He was looking at her again. Mark Wilson, the Call Centre Manager. The man Louise was going to marry. He didn't know yet. She'd made the decision the first day he walked into the office. He'd looked straight at Louise and smiled that wonderful smile. It was like a premonition. Her future flashed before her eyes. Mrs Louise Wilson – it sounded perfect.

It was Mark's first day back from leave. Louise couldn't take her eyes off him. He was even better looking with a suntan. It had been hell not seeing him for over two weeks. She had tried so hard not to think about him having fun with his family – and his wife.

When Louise found out that there was already a Mrs Wilson, and two junior Wilsons, it had initially seemed like a setback. Always suspicious of married men who didn't wear a wedding ring, Louise took the fact that Mark wore no ring as a sign that he was not totally committed. She had now convinced herself, it was just a matter of time before he realised he had made a mistake. Somehow Mrs Wilson would disappear, taking the two children with her of course, leaving Mark free to marry Louise. She knew he liked her. She could tell by the way he always looked straight at her when he walked into the office. Louise had told no one, not even her best friend Sally. Well there was nothing to tell – yet.

'Hello, my name is Louise. I'm representing a national company conducting a market research programme. If you agree to answer a few simple questions, you are automatically entered into a prize draw for a luxury holiday in the Caribbean. Would you like to answer a few questions – you would?'

Thank God for that, she thought.

The Call Centre had seemed a good choice. At first she was excited at the idea of working with new technology. Her Dad had said it was a job made for her.

'If our Lou's good at anything it's yapping on the telephone,' he'd say. Louise thought her Dad was a Male Chauvinist Pig – and he had no dress sense at all.

She looked over into Mark's office. He dressed immaculately. His clothes were always perfectly co-ordinated. She liked the way his shirt cuffs sneaked out from beneath his sleeves and revealed small but tasteful cufflinks. Not like her Dad's. His were loud and bright and only came out for Christmas or New Year parties.

Louise thought you could tell a lot about a man's personality by the clothes he wore. Her last boyfriend, Tony, wore the same two jumpers the whole three months they'd been together. Neither of which could have been described as stylish, co-ordinated or even tasteful. He probably didn't even own a suit. The leather jacket he always wore looked like it had been in armed combat.

Sometimes Louise imagined Mark in casual clothes. His dark hair curling over a beige cashmere polo neck sweater, dark brown chinos and a pair of real leather brogues. She had only ever seen him at work in his suits.

He would wear a grey morning suit when they got married. With a handmade silk shirt and a forget-me-not blue cravat that would exactly match the four bridesmaid's dresses. Sally would be Maid of Honour and her nieces, Emma, Jade and Carly would make beautiful bridesmaids. His two sons would be perfect page boys and would adore her when they saw her floating up the aisle in her Chanel dress.

Louise winced at the thought of her Dad walking her up the aisle. He was bound to say something to spoil it. He couldn't be any different. Louise didn't know why her Mum put up with him. He had been quite good looking when he was young. In their wedding photographs her Dad had long dark hair and a moustache. He looked so trendy in his turquoise jacket – like he was in one of those pop groups she'd seen on TOTP2. She'd better choose what he'd wear for her wedding, save a lot of embarrassment that way.

Louise fancied a honeymoon in the Caribbean, St Lucia or Tobago. She used to think Bermuda sounded exciting but Barry Manilow put her off that idea. Louise's eyes followed Mark as he strode out of the large office. She pictured them walking barefoot, hand in hand, on a white sandy beach. She had even considered exchanging marriage vows on a Caribbean beach. But she couldn't imagine getting married and not inviting all her family and friends.

'Hey Lou - are yer coming to the Pier tonight?' Hazel worked in sales and flounced into the office as if she owned the place. 'Carole, Vicky and Jools are going. We're all meeting at Carole's first for a little drinky poos to get us in the mood.'

Louise used to like going to the Pier but now she was bored with it. Hazel's getting really common just lately, she thought. Just look at her in those tight trousers. Makes her bum look like the winner of the Grand National.

'Can't. Said I'd babysit for our Paul. He's taking Sharon to the Multi-Screen.' She was becoming good at making up excuses. Louise smiled as Red Rum continued.

'Oh Lou – you never come out with us these days. Can't you ask yer Mam to do it?' One no was never enough for Hazel.

'Naw - Mam's Quiz night. She won't miss that.' That was true enough. Besides Tony would be at the Pier. She knew he wanted them to get together again. She couldn't tell him she was waiting for Mark. Louise sighed. Please – let it happen soon.

The phone rang. It was Veronica, Mark's PA. Louise distrusted Veronica. To be honest, she didn't like the stuck-up cow. The interruption at least sent Hazel packing with a 'see you later' wave.

'Mr Wilson would like to see you in his office – now.' Veronica's voice was cold and sharp. The word now reverberated in Louise's head.

'Wh... What right now?' This is it. Two weeks away and he knows that he can't live without me.

'Yes now – unless you're too busy of course.' Meow, meow mouthed Louise. She put down the headphones and straightened her hair. Should she nip to the loo, just to make sure her lipstick was still its vibrant Cherry Glow? No, she would have to pass Mark's office on the way. He'd see her and she didn't want to keep him waiting.

She took a deep breath and quietly knocked on the door. Her stomach felt like a hundred butterflies had taken flight. Louise sat opposite Mark; pleased she had worn her new black skirt. She'd taken ages to decide what to wear for Mark's first day back. Coyly she smoothed down the tight material. He gave her a quick smile and pulled at his ear lobe. She loved the way he did that when he was nervous.

'I've been watching you,' he said looking down at the papers on his desk.

I know you have, she thought, and I've been watching you, watching me.

'Do you like your job here at the Centre, Louise?' He was looking directly at her now. Perhaps he was going to ask her to leave because it would make life difficult once they started seeing each other. She had considered that too.

'It's just – well frankly you are well below our performance targets. This is the second month and there has been no improvement at all. In fact you are getting worse.'

Louise froze. Perhaps she had misheard. That cold she'd had last month had made her a bit deaf.

Mark continued. 'Every time I look over you seem to be on a different planet to the rest of us. The window gets more of your attention than anything else. Not everyone is suited to this type of work.' His blue eyes seemed much smaller today.

'I... I...' Louise found it impossible to speak. Her throat was closing in on her. She coughed to give herself time to think. She looked around the room wanting the ground to open and swallow her up. She saw the photographs. Happy family photographs; children with big smiles and missing teeth. And then she looked down, for once stunned into silence. Her eyes lingered on his socks. She was devastated. It would never have worked. Louise knew that now. She could never marry anyone who wore white socks with a dark suit.

The Reading
RON GEDDES

Arthur J W McDoubleday was, from his birth, bestowed with every element of physical and emotional meanness. From an early age, publishing and selling scandal newssheets, later, he took on the jobs other students shunned, such as writing dissertations for them and withholding them until the last moment, so extorting many times more than the agreed fee. His philosophy was that the best way to double your money was to fold it over in your pocket.

With dour Scottish parents, he neither received nor gave any love or affection, nor had he received or given a kiss, hug or touch to anyone or thing. No stranger to violence in the pursuit of materialism, it was no surprise that when both his parents died in a suspicious fire, he left the country, leaving them to the ignominy of a pauper's funeral.

After having eked a third cup of tea from a bag, he snarled when his phone rang. It was his uncle's solicitor, Harold Hackenbush, requesting a meeting.

Once arrived and seated, Arthur always accepted free tea, the better with biscuits. When sated, the lawyer commenced.

'Thank you for coming, Mr. McDoubleday. As you know

your uncle died without issue, leaving his estate to any surviving niece and/or nephew. We've taken some time to search for your cousin Morag Templeton. From what you told us, we traced her to Tobago where she owned and operated a scuba diving school … which, from what we gleaned, was very successful and profitable. However, she has disappeared. The police suspect foul play and involvement with drugs. Nevertheless, it's taken a while to apply to the court to declare her deceased for the purposes of administering the will.'

The police were not aware Morag was never involved with drugs but she suspected many of her customers were. Some were just users but others were heavily into manufacture and distribution, much of the latter above and below the water line. Notwithstanding, their relationships were always friendly, each offering often to call the other if ever help was needed.

Arthur's eyes were piggy with greed. His uncle Andrew was his idol, his business interests, legal and otherwise, valuable and extensive. Arthur sat demurely, resisting the once in a lifetime urge to jump up with glee. Secretly and smugly he believed he had got away with it, the result justifying the cost. Briefly his thoughts went to how he killed his cousin.

It was a plan worthy of a KGB assassination. Travelling to Willemstad in the Netherlands Antilles, an innocent, one of many yacht charters along the northern coast of South America, resulted in an overnight stay off Anse Fourmi, a small fishing village on the north coast Of Tobago. At dusk it was easy for Arthur to go ashore without paperwork, to ostensibly visit a local bar. Once ashore, using a small motor cycle he brought along, he rode to his cousin's house, located above the dive shop.

It was just dark when he entered. The day's business was finished and apart from the owner, the place was empty. The tall athletically built, blond haired woman looked at him with contempt for a man not even worthy of her spittle.

'Hello Morag, longtime no see. How are you?'

She said nothing, mentally the friendship had ended a long time ago. In fact, realistically, it had never begun, their association only improving with absence and separation. He continued.

'I'm on a yacht cruise. Just parked in the next bay. Couldn't pass without saying hello. Drink?'

He produced a bottle of Longmorn 1967 single malt scotch from a bag. Two glasses allowed them to appreciate the nectar in the bitterness of the moment. It was when Morag left the room that Arthur spiked her glass. Soon, she was awake but incapable of movement.

'Arthur, I'm feeling bad,' she said.

'Oh. Must have been dirty ice in the drinks.'

She became more and more incoherent.

He watched as she succumbed deeper, until he judged the time right. Then, lifting her bodily he took her to the end of the jetty where her dive boats were moored. It was an unusual show of pity when he carefully slipped her into the water and held her head under. After what seemed an appropriate time he released his pressure and was satisfied as she sunk away. Thereafter, he returned to the house and cleaned away any evidence of his presence and returned to the yacht. That was twelve months ago.

The solicitor was about to ask Arthur to sign the documents for transferring his uncle's assets to him, when a flustered secretary barged in. Hackenbush was outraged.

'You know not to interrupt me when I'm with a client. What do you want?'

'There's someone to see you.'

'Do they have an appointment?'

'No, but I think you'll want to see this one.'

There was no comment until a tall woman, dressed goth like in a long black floor length coat, with a pale face, bright red lipstick and black as pitch spiked hair entered. It was a guise that would elevate Lisbeth Salander's envy to catastrophic heights.

Notwithstanding that she had made an excellent job of the change, Arthur recognised his cousin. She's back, he thought.

'Who are you?' asked lawyer Hackinbush.

'Morag Templeton.'

There was a pause. From deep in a large bag, the woman produced a montage of photos before and after, DNA certificates and passports, pre and post goth.

'Some paper proving who I am.' She turned and sneeringly smiled at Arthur.

'And of course, my dear, dear cousin Arthur will confirm who I am. Won't you?'

There was no sound.

'Cat got your tongue? A nod will do. NOW! We don't want to hold the lawyer up, do we?'

With open mouth, Arthur complied, his concern absolute.'

'So what happened to you? Where have you been?' asked the lawyer. 'We've been trying to find you.'

'Oh, simple. I think I had too much to drink one night and fell into the water at the end of the jetty at my Tobago house. I lost consciousness and my memory for a while. I think it's all on the CD disc from the CCTV I installed to catch people who were stealing from me.'

Arthur was so worried he thought his heart would stop. But it did not. Having no control and with the possibility of not only losing half of his inheritance but being incarcerated in jail was a shock. But it was also a catalyst to do something as soon as possible. He doubted Morag would join him for another drink.

The cousins listened to the lawyer, explaining what would now happen. Arthur seethed and Morag gloated. He wanted out to return home to his comforts and contacts, to make sure next time, Morag would be properly and finally disposed of. Perhaps, he thought, it was time to call in the loan he gave to the local funeral director, who conveniently had a functioning crematorium. Morag's dust on the waters would be final and untraceable.

Arthur opened his front door and from behind, was seized and pushed forward. As he felt something hard and small like the end of a pistol barrel hard against his head, a deep voice with an accent resembling Bob Marley, spoke.

'Don't turn around!'

Two things happened quickly. He noticed the entrance was covered floor to ceiling with plastic sheeting. It was shades of Dexter Morgan and his thoughts were interrupted by Morag's voice.

'It's a good thing I can hold my breath for so long, cousin. It comes from free diving, I'm good for near five minutes. Too bad you won't have the chance to try it.'

Morag nodded to the Tobagian gunman she imported and the hammer retracted.

A Lost Secret
ALAN GILBERT

Grampy, my paternal grandfather, was a quiet and digni-fied man. He never argued, never raised his voice and, to a ten-year-old boy, didn't seem a lot of fun until, that is, we began playing draughts. In this game, with its deceptively simple rules, he became alert, jolly and unbeatable. My father had introduced me to the game and played against me many times until I managed to win. The first time I defeated my father was also the last, since he avoided playing again, but as much as I improved my game I never once bettered Grampy.

My grandparents' home was a semi-detached house, constructed in the 1930's and had a large living room, looking out onto the rear garden, with a similar sized room at the front. The latter was carpeted, had a three piece suite and piano. This was a special place and rarely used. Grandma was always busy washing clothes, baking, harvesting fruit or making jam for the chapel that, somehow, she never attended. Grampy, though, marched off every Sunday wearing his best suit and precisely positioned bowler hat, to take his place in the choir.

In 1914, Grampy had gone to war leaving two young children and a pregnant wife. Rather oddly he had remained with the army, in Germany, for two years after the war had ended, long after everyone else had returned. I learned to ask Grampy questions only when we were alone and as the 1950's became the 1960's I realized that he really could understand the German language and seemed to like, and even admire, the German people. I found this rather surprising and became very curious, but didn't know how to phrase the questions that constantly rumbled in my mind.

They were a great team, my grandparents, but mention the war and the whole house seemed to freeze. I came to learn that he had stayed with a German family and sometimes mumbled a feminine name before seeming to shrink into his chair and leave my world for a while. I would always respect his space and go for a chat with Grandma. There were other grandchildren, of course, but my favourite was Christine. A year younger than me, she was attractive, outspoken and pulled no punches. She was a brilliant dancer, trendy, worldly and 'with it.' Unfortunately, none of these attributes came close to describing me.

Then there was Jayne. We had grown up in the same street. She was blonde; blue eyed and, as each year passed, became increasingly stunning. As young children, we played and enjoyed each other's company until puberty began to erode our childhood. We had both attended the same infants' school but in different classes since I was a year older. At seven years of age we progressed to single sex, all-age schools which were adjacent to each other. Then there was the dreaded Eleven Plus examination. This was compulsory and the few successful children would transfer to a coeducational grammar school. It could be quite depressing for the rest of us though, since we had to remain at the same school until the age of fifteen.

There was one well remembered day though. Jayne had to pass my home on her way to school and on that day, I was suddenly aware of a blonde girl, wearing a red mackintosh, just standing still at the corner of our street.

'Are you okay Jayne?' I asked quietly. She shook her head slowly.

'What is it?' I asked. The clumsy question made her begin to cry.

'The exam,' she mumbled quietly.

Being a year older I was well aware of the pressure that adults sometimes exerted on their children and the inevitable boastful demeanour exhibited by many parents of the chosen ones, but I tried to smile and said, 'I failed and I'm OK. It doesn't really matter.' The lie came easily, 'Come on, I'll walk with you.'

Luckily, she began to walk but with obvious reluctance. I normally allowed only the minimum time to get to school, any delay would result in my arriving late but Jayne was very special. I then did something that, for me, was quite outrageous. I took her hand and waited for it to be pulled away. It wasn't. We walked hand in hand right up to the girls' entrance. Jayne was going to be late, but only just, and they wouldn't have started the tortuous inquisition just yet. An unpleasant fate awaited me, though, but I cared little.

'Remember, it doesn't matter that much,' I said, unable to think of anything better. I released her hand and waited until she reached the end of the short corridor leading into the school. She looked back for an instant and was gone. We never spoke of this event, even though she also failed, but I was somehow bewitched and whenever our paths crossed my brain simply disintegrated and refused to allow any intelligent speech whatsoever. As time moved on, other aspiring boy-friends appeared to have no such problems. She was a popular girl.

It became apparent that successful males were smarmy and had acquired a special language. A smile and brief word compelled girls to giggle and a whisper in their ear made them dissolve. My handicap was not limited to communications. There was much more. My parents believed that I should dress exactly as my father had during the bizarre decade that preced-ed World War Two. In an age when every other young male sported drainpipe trousers I was sentenced to baggy ones. Then there was dancing. Girls expected their boyfriends to be able to jive, a vital skill denied to me but generously awarded to everyone else.

During my last year at school I noticed that Jayne had become friendly with Carol. She lived a couple of streets away and was a grammar school girl. Such superior beings rarely mixed with lesser mortals and I became apprehensive about this development since Carol was an extremely well developed girl, constantly seen snogging with grammar school boys, even at lunchtime. Was the object of my constant affection going to be drawn into this world? It was also rumoured that both intended to become hairdressers. I would often see them together and one evening, as I looked out of my bedroom window, they jogged by, identically dressed in green sweaters and blue slacks. My eyes followed them until they disappeared from view. Jayne was so near yet so completely beyond my reach.

Days later I was walking behind and gaining on the pair as they approached a crossroads. I was within inches of Jayne and determined to speak when I was suddenly rendered invisible as two tall, and very good looking, males approached from the left. Both girls began waving before rushing towards these hateful aliens. I had been eclipsed and at that moment gave up all hope. The intruders were, in fact, privately educated boarders home for the holidays. A worldlier me would have realized that it was Jayne and Carol who were out of their depth.

I left school at the age of 15 and as the years passed by I dated a few girls and even had steady relationships but in my late teens I had once again entered into a state of disunion. I wasn't courting, as my elders quaintly put it, and found the concept of flirting quite incomprehensible. One day though, in my favourite bookshop, everything changed. As I carelessly disturbed a book on the top shelf, it nearly rendered unconscious someone studying at the lower levels. As the inevitable apology was uttered I found myself ambushed by those never forgotten blue eyes, and they were smiling.

For a few seconds, the well remembered inability to speak swamped my mind. I was frozen, unable to utter a sound but, slowly, the newer more experienced me struggled to free himself from the spell and finally, managed to suggest coffee. This grew into lunch and we instantly became an item. Nearly four months of exhilarating bliss followed but I was seriously deluding myself since a gorgeous creature such as Jayne needed a boyfriend as others needed earrings. Was I becoming paranoid or was she finding me increasingly boring?

Jayne, unlike former girlfriends, had never uttered a single criticism concerning me and, one wet and cold day, she began to extol my virtues. This kindness, so completely unexpected, began to develop a deep feeling of unease and when she explained that we had no future together I was almost able to conceal my misery. I could cope with the resulting humiliation but when Jayne moved out of my life everything seemed meaningless and my enfeebled mind seemed to be shrivelling.

When a concerned Grandma quietly asked how things were, I was too embarrassed to share my misery and didn't know what to say. Grampy, however, was about to surprise me. We no longer played draughts together or discussed worldly matters and I was somewhat bewildered by his sudden and unforeseen suggestion.

'Grandma needs a little space for her baking so shall we go for a walk?'

It was the type of day that you really are supposed to encounter in March and we faced a noisy headwind immediately after leaving the house. Within the confines of his home I had not registered Grampy's growing frailty but, as we entered a wood and moved along a path towards the river, I became increasingly concerned as the trees noisily tried to resist the overwhelming forces thrown against them. Grampy brushed my protests aside.

We talked little to begin with, probably because neither of us knew how to start but, without warning, he stopped, looked me straight in the eye and asked, 'Are you feeling better?'

I was uncertain as to his meaning and probably looked rather baffled, so he continued: 'Walking is good for you, it somehow lessens the pain.'

I was a little confused. I had never been able to discuss problems with anyone, particularly my family, and had become accustomed to presenting a confident facade to the world.

'I understand pain,' he continued, 'Grief can spill out of your mind and smother every moment of your life, but walking helps you to see things more clearly.'

Jayne was no longer the dominant thought in my mind. Grampy's simple wisdom had squeezed all personal worries from my head and I was taken back through time to long for-gotten conversations. The distant, half remembered, name tried to scramble into my foggy conscious mind. Grampy seemed to sense my growing confusion and continued,

'We all experience despair and for me it will remain until I die and,' he hesitated for a moment, 'Perhaps beyond, but yours will pass, believe me it will pass.'

He said so much more as things began to surface in my awakening mind.

'At this moment we are sharing a journey,' he continued,' something we do not do very often. Jayne is a very attractive and lovely girl and you have been sharing a journey together but now she wants to go a different way.'

'You mean she finds me boring?'

'No. Have you discussed your plans and hopes for the future?'

By now I wasn't thinking about me. I wanted to question him but couldn't find the courage and so simply answered his question.

'Well yes, of course.'

'There you are then; she just doesn't share your hopes. Jayne wants to take a different route through life.'

'Of course, how can I have been so stupid? I should have tried to explore her ambitions more.'

'No, that wouldn't have helped at all.'

'What do you mean?'

'Jayne is a sensible and pleasant girl with simple ambitions, like most people really, but you have quite complicated ideas which will take time and may not even work. Dreams need to be shared.'

He said so much more but I remember one poignant moment when he said,

'Quite soon, you will realize that you have been a very lucky man. Jayne is not only sensible but honest. Never be in a hurry to find a wife and always try to remember that should you make such an enormous mistake you cannot let someone else suffer because of it.'

He paused for a moment before adding as he looked away,

'Whatever we do is going to hurt someone, though, including ourselves.'

'I'm not sure what you mean,' I replied but, even as I spoke, I knew he was talking about himself.

'It will come to you in time.'

'But you and Grandma?'

He lifted his hand to silence me.

'Your grandmother is a wonderful woman and we have been through a lot together.'

The subject was closed but I kept wondering about how long it took him to return home after the war and, of course, that name.

At the age of twenty five I had long since found my soul mate and was living contentedly some hundred miles distant from my parents, but whenever I talked to my cousin Christine, we would always reminisce about times spent with our grandparents. One day, though, Christine telephoned me to explain how our parents were considering placing the two of them in a residential home. We shared the unhappy realization that this would be the end, but we were frustratingly powerless.

They didn't survive long in the home. Grampy died first followed, a few weeks later, by Grandma and, soon after her funeral, Christine telephoned me with the news that she had surprised my parents throwing Grampy's diaries onto a bonfire. There had been one diary for each year of his life following the return from Germany. There were also small notebooks and I felt privileged to have read some of the neatly printed short poems that were dispersed throughout the diaries and books but, always felt that there was much more hiding within them.

I was frantic. Questioning my parents would certainly have driven them to move with more haste but, until the weekend, I was powerless. Two sleepless nights followed but by Saturday morning I was at my parents' house, appearing relaxed and saying nothing of my concerns. It is my experience that following a death, some relatives can take on the characteristics of those long necked birds, routinely seen in old western films, which circle overhead waiting for their emaciated victims to die. Unlike vultures the human driving force is not the simple need to eat but acquisitiveness and greed. I could not predict the behaviour of my immediate relatives but Grampy had a beautiful pre-war radio and an amazing postcard collection which had begun with items assembled in France and Germany. I, along with my cousins, loved gazing at the cards but knew that the fate of these items would not be decided by us.

My concerns lay elsewhere and so I said little and refrained from revealing my thoughts and just listened. We travelled separately to the old house and as I slowly drifted around imagining Grampy, still in his favourite chair and Grandma baking and making jam, it became apparent that everyone else had moved upstairs. A number of old rectangular biscuit tins were spread carelessly around the living room table, their former contents, I knew, were already ash but I was still drawn to the cupboard where they had rested for so long. As I opened the door my heart shuddered to a halt. At the very bottom of the old cupboard, two tin boxes remained. I hardly dared touch them and closed the cupboard door before walking back into the hallway. Everyone was still rummaging upstairs.

Could these old tins still hold any diaries? I returned quickly to the cupboard, reached down with trembling hands, raised the ageing containers and quietly removed the lids. Among old precious photographs were two overlooked old military notebooks. I opened each one, very carefully, with a feeling of enormous anticipation. Squeezed between Magnetism and Morse was one poem. Between Cables and Electricity was another. One piece took me back to my childhood and another to our special walk. Was this the one I wondered? I quietly removed these precious items of treasure, together with some photographs and, after carefully replacing everything else, moved my discoveries to the safety of my car.

Strolling around the garden I was overwhelmed by happy images of my grandparents and it seemed appropriate to take my leave. I could sense my parent's relief as I said my goodbyes.

During the years that have passed since that time, life has thrown up many challenges and it is then that I feel the need to walk, but when the wind's brute force crashes its way through the captive trees I think of Grampy and still wonder, did a secret die with him or did it live on with someone in that foreign land, which my parents and grandparents had fought against, for just a few more years? Sometimes I think of Jayne, our happy childhood and the mistakes I could have so easily made, but that takes me back to Grampy.

A Tudor Life
DENISE LIGHT

In the second year in the reign of King Henry Tudor there happened the largest storm that had been seen in living memory. It laid waste to many of the fields and animals which left people throughout the land without the means to survive.

Often the young men took to scavenging the hedgerows and woods but woe betide them if they were caught poaching in their lords demesne. Wailing and tears were often to be heard in villages in the north, in the south and in between, where a young man had been summarily dealt with.

But then there came salvation, or so it seemed at the time. A messenger came, from the king himself, telling all of the great ships he was building and of how they would be used to fight the French. He asked for men throughout the land to join in this endeavour.

And so it was that young men came to Portsmouth thinking they would be able to find work on the great ships. And some did, but for most it simply led to a life, and subsequent death, at sea.

One young man, Matthew Walton, had walked for two days from his village to find the great ships. A skilled carpenter he was but with little work at home he decided to seek his fortune elsewhere. And now he found himself looking in wonder at the ship being built in front of his eyes.

King Henry's great ship was the largest construction he had ever seen. A huge ship with three decks and four masts. Matthew found the foreman and soon found himself taken on.

And from then on Matthew's days were taken up with sawing and fixing the great planks into place. Sometimes he looked at the great trees that were delivered to the shipyard and wondered just how many would be left in the land when the king had finished his ships. He himself had lost count of the number he had worked on. Somebody said 600 oak trees and some elm had been felled for this single ship.

Matthew found for himself a lodging house not far from the shipyard. From here he ventured out to the local hostelry. Not every night; sometimes he would just walk along the sea shore. And it was on one of these walks that he met Annie. She and her mother often went down to the seashore to see what they could find. Annie's father had died the previous year so the two of them would go scavenging as a way of getting some money.

After that Matthew spent less time in the hostelry and more time on the seashore. And it seemed sensible that he should become their lodger for they did not have one at that time. The day Annie announced she was pregnant was the day Matthew said they should wed. A month later they were married at St Mary's.

Matthew was a happy man. He had come from a poor existence and now found himself with a wife and a child on the way. He had a job he loved. His passion was working the wood on the great ship. He felt a real affinity with it and occasionally, when no one was looking, he put his own mark on the planks. Matthew's days were taken up by making the King's dream turn into reality.

Finally in July 1511 came the day when the big ship was launched and the men who had toiled over the hull and fixed the planks in place could see it in all its glory. Well not quite all, because she still needed fitting out. Matthew's chest filled with pride when he looked on his work. The King had named his ship Mary Rose and after the launch it was sailed to London to be fitted with the decking, rigging and armaments.

Matthew expected that to be the last time he would see the great ship. But he had proved himself to be a good worker and so continued to labour on other ships being built for King Henry's navy.

Matthew's wife presented him with a daughter and he called her after the ship for it was the Mary Rose that had brought him and his wife together. Mary was followed by Henry and six other children. He loved them all and was grateful that he was able to provide for them. As the years went by he became one of the most trusted workers in the shipyard and his work and responsibility increased along with the money he earned.

So busy was the shipyard that in 1527 a new dock was dug at Portsmouth. And, 16 years after she had left, the Mary Rose sailed into that new dock where she was caulked and repaired. Matthew was pleased that he was now a proper shipwright. This time the back-breaking work of cutting new planks for the hull or decking was not for him. But once more he watched her sail off expecting never to see the great ship again.

But he was wrong. Once more the Mary Rose returned to Portsmouth. And once again Matthew worked on her. Much of the great ship was very different to the ship he had helped to build all those years before.

His son, Henry, was now working in the yard keen to follow in his father's footsteps. As they walked home after working on the ship all day, Henry & his father discussed the altered ship.

Matthew had been looking all round the ship during the time she was in dock. 'I think all these alterations are not good for the ship. I don't think she's as stable as she used to be and I am sure she's not as quick as previously.'

Henry looked at his father, whose opinion he greatly admired, 'Do you think she will be all right? Or will we have more work to do?'

'I don't know, son. This is the third time I have worked on her. Maybe she will return again.'

And then there came that most awful of days. Matthew

had come to Portsmouth all those years before to help build ships to fight the French. In 1545 they were still fighting them and the Mary Rose was often at the forefront. On the 19th July in that year she led the attack on the French fleet in what became known as the Battle of the Solent. The French were intending to land troops to invade England so the King himself had come to Portsmouth to see his ships in action.

Matthew and his sons were part of the crowd that watched the battle from the shore. Matthew was always keen to see his favourite ship and he was now able to see the Mary Rose in action.

'Look father, they are going to shoot, the gun ports are open.'

'Yes, son. They are the ones on the main deck that have only been added in recent years.' Matthew would always be able to tell his sons some of the finer details of the Mary Rose. 'I think they made the openings too low.'

As they watched they saw the great ship start to turn. It was a sharp turn and she tipped over and the watchers could see water pour over the side and into the gun ports.

'Oh father, look what's happening, she's going down,' said William, his younger son.

'I do hope she isn't,' said his father, 'But I think you are right, it is so windy she is unable to right herself and there is now so much water going in. I have a really bad feeling.'

And Matthew decided that he didn't want to see the end

of his ship, the Mary Rose, the ship he had started on over 30 years before. And he turned and trudged home, grieving for the ship, for the king and all the men who lost their lives that day.

Postscript

The next time the world was to see the Mary Rose was in October 1982 when it was raised to the surface of the Solent. There was no King to see the salvage but our Prince of Wales was there to see the Mary Rose break the surface for the first time in over 400 years.

Since then the wooden timbers of the hull have been undergoing conservation. I would like to think that many of those planks were worked on by Matthew Walton and perhaps his mark might one day be found.

Refuge
GAIL LITTLEFAIR

Urine soaked mattress, holes in the door.
This drunken behaviour, I can't take much more.
My children at risk, of his drunken state.
My Son packs my bags, he is only eight.

Under Police escort, we are taken away.
The children are stressed, they don't want to play.
What keeps you going, when life falls apart?
No one to love, you've broken your heart.

The strength of your love, for a Daughter and Son,
encourages you to take, each day as it comes.
Living within the four walls of your home.
Anxious, depressed, frightened, alone.

Downhearted, despairing, facing life on your own.
There's no silver lining, not even a bone.
I hope when they're grown, they will see,
nothing was for gain; nothing was for me.

The reason why, I did what I did?
I did what I did, for the love of my kids.

A Child's Cry
CHRISTINE McCRAE

A final breath and then she was gone. For ever. Finished, silenced, never to speak about her memories, laugh at the TV, or cry at a weepy film again. Dead. Aunt Alice was ninety years old. She spent the last eleven years in a home.

'A good age,' said the undertaker sympathetically. 'Good health until the last few weeks. A good innings.'

I was her only relative now since her sister, Peggy, died. The will was already lodged with the solicitor, so they started the probate process. Six months later I was the proud owner of a 17th century manor house called 'The Olde Hall.' It was in the centre of the hamlet of Long Rake in the deepest Derbyshire Peak District.

Arriving at the house I was shocked at the state of disrepair. No one had been here for years. The garden was choked with nettles and brambles; ivy clung to the walls and door and the windows were covered with years of grime and cobwebs. I picked my way down the uneven flags to the weather beaten front door. Once, it had been a handsome home but now it looked crumbling and derelict. The gritstone façade and period mullion windows looked sad, heavy, and neglected.

'Are you family?' asked the cheerful, red-faced woman next door.

'I'm the new owner. My Aunt Alice passed away last year and I have inherited the property,' I replied.

'Well duckie, no one has crossed that threshold for many years. Not since your Aunt Alice and Aunt Peggy were here. Just watch your step in there.'

'I can see it looks neglected. I'm going to have a lot to do. '

'You're not on your own are you?'

'Well I am actually, but I'll be ok'

'Not to worry you, but it will be a bit creepy in there. If you need any help let us know.'

Maybe I should have persuaded my friend Sam to come, but she was going to a wedding and had a busy weekend planned. So here I am sorting it out myself.

I took out a bunch of keys. Surely one would fit. After twenty minutes of trying, SUCCESS! The front door groaned and shuddered as it swung open. Spiders scuttled here and there. A mountain of post slid across the tiled floor with the movement of the door. Years of unopened mail. A smell of stale air and something I couldn't quite place hit me as I stepped inside. The old fashioned furniture was grey and dusty. Everywhere was festooned with thick cobwebs. The atmosphere was heavy and unpleasant. It was untidy, almost as if someone had left in a rush. There was a bookcase in one corner. I bent down to look closer. It held many well-loved books including the Classics and Shakespeare, some were leather bound. On the bottom shelf were a couple of diaries. I brushed the dust off to see the date. 1943 and 44. War time recordings. Imagine that, Aunt Alice's recordings of wartime years.

My idea was to stay a night or two to have a good look at the place and see what there was. I found the water stop tap and the fuse box so I had basic services. Next I set to work to make the place a little cleaner for my short stay.

As I worked, I realised there must be a cellar under the house. I noticed a door almost hidden at the back of the bookcase. I dragged the bookcase a little aside. The door was locked with a hefty padlock. One of my keys opened it but despite much pushing and shoving it wouldn't move. I gave it a massive kick, hoping the wood wouldn't splinter. It moved slightly. Something seemed to be holding it shut. What a struggle I had with it. Eventually, it gave in. It moved and creaked heavily and swung open. Foul, icy cold air swirled up into my face. I was taken aback. Something rustled down there. Mice maybe, or worse. I could see the first few steps but the rest was pitch black. I felt something brush past my face and over my right shoulder, but I didn't see anything. I was terrified. I jumped up and slammed the door shut. What was it? It was definitely spooky in this house. I tried to calm myself down and be rational. This was simply an old house which had been shut up for many years. I decided to explore the cellar properly some other time.

I spent the next couple of hours preparing a small bedroom where I planned to spend the night. Several times, I felt that cool breeze waft past my face. Was something strange going on or was this just a draughty house?

I got into my sleeping bag fully clothed. If it all got too much and I needed to escape at least I could make a quick getaway. I lit a lamp at the side of my makeshift bed. It cast dancing shadows on the walls which made me nervous.

'Don't be a fool,' I thought. 'Nothing will hurt you here.'

After two hours of fitful sleep, I thought I could hear a new born baby crying in the distance. There it was again. It sounded real. In fact it seemed to be in the house. My body felt tense. I felt sick with fear now. My heart was banging so much that the sound filled my head. I sat up and looked around. The furniture formed ghostly shapes in the room. Suddenly, in one corner, I saw the unmistakable figure of a woman in a white dress with a new baby in her arms sitting in a rocking chair. The baby was whimpering quietly and the woman was gazing silently at it. I felt the hairs go up on the back of my neck and I was numb with fear. My God, what was happening? Then in the space of three seconds the image slowly faded away. Completely disappeared. I had experienced a ghost! This place was haunted!

There was a creak on the stairs. Was someone in the house? I lay there paralysed with fear for some time. I couldn't stay in this house, it was haunted! I gathered some stuff together and set up a bed in the back of my car. Gazing back at the house I thought what a scary place it was turning out to be. What was that at the window? It was the woman in white with the babe in her arms. She was looking sadly across the garden. Maybe she wanted the house for herself. She was a spirit attached to the house for some reason.

I touched the gold cross I always wore around my neck. It always seemed protective. I said a prayer for the distraught spirit and also for myself.

Early the next day I spoke to Annie next door about my bad night.

'Yes, it is supposed to be haunted. I didn't know whether to tell you. It might have frightened you. There was a good chance you might not have seen anything anyway. Alice and Peggy were always a bit of a mystery. Reclusive in their later years.'

I decided to get back home and consult an expert on what to do next but first I went back in the house. I wanted to look at Aunt Alice's diaries. She might have written about the ghost. However there was no mention of ghosts. In the diary for 1943 she was very effusive about a two-week romance with an American serviceman. This was during World War 2 of course. Then in December she wrote *Pregnant. Told Peggy.'* So she must have had a baby around the following August. There it was in 1944, August: *'Gave birth to a boy. Terrible struggle. Only me and Peggy.'*

She must have given birth secretly in this house with no medical help. She was too scared and maybe ashamed, as women in her situation may have been then. Days later we have the tragic entry *'Poor baby – buried in cellar.'*

So it was all clear. Alice gave birth secretly and her baby is buried down in the cellar. What a terrible thing to have hidden all these years. No wonder the house felt heavy and haunted.

I locked up and set off home. The ghosts are now free to roam at will but one day I will return with someone who can lay these spirits to rest and let them be at peace.

Fun By Moonlight
PAULINE MURDOCH

The clock struck twelve and Connor knew his Mum and Dad would be asleep. It was a moonlit night so he had no trouble in finding his dressing gown and slippers and creeping down the stairs. He saw something sparkling at the end of the garden and he wanted to find out what it was. Silently he stood on tip toe and opened the back door.

The trees moved a little bit in the breeze and made ghostly shadows on the garden. Connor moved slow down the path pulling his dressing gown closer and peering into the gloom. Just then a snail popped up and said 'Psst Pstt!' Connor stopped surprised and bent over the snail. 'Mind the plant,' said the snail. 'It has poisonous blue pellets around it.'

'Oh' said Connor 'Thank you for warning me.'

A little mouse yawned and stretched himself. 'Don't touch the mushrooms,' he said, 'I know they make you sick.'

'Oh' said Connor. 'Oh, I see –' and he looked really puzzled because he had never heard a mouse speak before. He moved forward towards the wild flower border.

Just at the edge of the border on the buddleia bush were some blue butterflies. Connor bent down to see if they were asleep. The large butterfly stretched his wings and yawned. 'Don't eat the deadly-nightshade,' he said. 'It is very bad for you.'

'I sat on it once,' the smallest butterfly said, 'and I thought I would die.'

Connor didn't know what to say, he was so surprised by what he heard. Then a tiny butterfly woke up and stretched her wings, she shook herself and, standing up tall her wings spread out, she turned into a blue fairy, her fair hair falling down her back. 'Follow me,' she said, 'and I will show you the magic pool.'

She picked up her wand and they set off towards the end of the garden where there was a little pond surrounded by a path. They walked quietly round the path and the fairy pointed to the goldfish swimming in the water – like little gold lights. A frog sat on a lily pad and let out a croak. It made Connor jump. 'You must see this,' the fairy went on. 'Follow me.'

They followed the path to the vegetable patch. Past the rows of cabbages and carrots and along the rows of beans and at the very end in the corner, sitting on a post, there was a little gnome. He wore a red jersey and green trousers and had a white beard.

'What are you doing in my kingdom?' he asked a startled Connor. 'What do you want?'

Connor's eyes were large with amazement. 'I don't want anything, I didn't know you were here,' he said. 'I was just looking round.'

'Well, stop disturbing me,' the angry gnome shouted. 'I am trying to rest. If you come here again, I will tie you up!'

Connor was frightened and held tightly to the fairy's hand. 'Don't worry,' she said. 'I can cast a spell on that old gnome and turn him into a stone statue!'

'Could you really do that?' Connor asked in surprise.

'Oh easy,' she said 'What shall I make him into? A stone animal or a toad? Whatever you want, I can do it with my magic wand!'

Just at that moment it started to rain, large drops fell on Connor's head. The fairy said she would have to go or else her wings would get too wet. 'Shall I magic you back home?' she asked. Connor couldn't believe it was possible but she whispered a spell and waved her wand and hey presto! Connor was back in his room, all tucked up in his little bed, and he could hear the rain pattering on the window. No matter how hard he tried he couldn't see the fairy or the gnome in the garden. Even the snail and the mouse were nowhere to be seen the next morning.

He didn't tell anyone about his adventures because he knew grown-ups never believed in children's stories.

They say: 'You must have been dreaming...'

Prose. Mary Magdalene 1840s
MANDY PULLEN

As I walk down this dim lit street, I feel the darkness creep towards me from either side of the narrow brick walls. The cobbles under my boot press against the arch of my foot as I place one foot in front of the other. I look down at my boots that once was; my big toe protruding from its worn-out leather the toe nail looks gnarled and dirty. I arrive at my destination at the end of this street. The gas lamp above my head flickers and blinks as the wind blows through the cracks of the broke glass and I think the flame will blow out leaving me stood here, in the cold and darkness.

Then I feel its wetness first on the tip of my nose, then on my lashes, I raise my eyes to the sky and they begin to fall, small ones at first, then big fat pretty ones that twinkle as they pass by me and gently flutter to the ground.

I pull the shawl around my head and shoulders tight, to keep the warmth in and the snow out.   I begin to feel the cold seep through to my bones making me shiver as the tiny hairs on the back of my arms stand to attention.

As I wait the snow begins to fall thicker and faster, I say to myself I will wait another few minutes and if he doesn't arrive with the tuppence owed, I will turn around and go back from where I came.

Then I see a stranger. He slowly walks towards me; there appears to be a light shining around him.

As he gets nearer, I can see his dark eyes and long straight nose, he smiles and his face lights up. He holds out his hand asking me to take it even though I cannot see his lips move.

I reach out to touch his hand and stumble, before I fall to the path, he is there holding me tight against his chest, I can feel his heart beating and his warmth; I do not want to move from this moment.

He answers to my thoughts and tells me this moment will last forever if I take his hand and follow him.

He looks into my face and his eyes penetrate deep into mine and I know I am with him.

We walk hand in hand back down the cobbled path and my feet feel no pain, my big toe looks pink

and clean.

As we walk along this path, he tells me his name and how his mother and father travelled on a donkey over a desert of sands to a town called Bethlehem. He said his mother had given birth to him in a stable.

He said that day had been a special day named Christmas Day, He also tells me today is Christmas Day and is a very special day for me.

Mother's Day
MARY SIMPSON

Liz put her coffee on the small table and sat down heavily in the armchair. I'm so tired, I shouldn't be, haven't achieved much this morning.

She sank in the chair, her eyes felt heavy and she felt hot; her head began to drop towards her chest. She brought her head up with a start. Goodness.

She took a sip of her coffee, ah, that's better. Jack was playing golf this morning; she was going to meet him for lunch at the golf club but that was in a couple of hours, she had plenty of time for a nap and there was no one else likely to call.

No Mother's Day flowers or cards. Her boys were both dead. The tears started and she was leaden as she sank further into the chair and her eyes closed.

She felt herself rising out of her body. She looked down as she rose, surprise registering as she saw below her the neat well dressed woman with short blond hair and a drawn, worn out look on her face.

She was amazed at her calmness, was she dead? Was she dreaming?

She knew she was still grieving for her boys, both killed

in Afghanistan, Matthew 5 years ago and Ian last year. There had been no real joy since their deaths, but today was more poignant because they had always made it so special for her. Even when they were students, they always managed to make it home for Mother's Day.

She seemed to be travelling or moving and she was coming into light. She appeared to be in full warm sunshine, the place wherever it was looked beautiful. There were majestic buildings that seemed to glow in the pure wonderful light. There were people too. Happy looking, brightly dressed, the colours of the clothing vivid, luminous.

She walked along a road which led her into a park where the grass was verdant and a lake that shimmered reflecting this beautiful light and the sky was pure magic, she had never seen blue so vibrant before.

She kept walking, she could hear music and in the distance she could see a band stand and the strains of an orchestra reaching her ears was exquisite, touching her heart and making her content. She felt marvellous.

She had reached the bandstand and stood there listening with a small crowd of smiling people. She felt a touch on her right shoulder. She turned and there was her son, Matthew. A lighter hand on her other shoulder and there was Ian.

It seemed natural as she hugged them both.

There were no words, they were not needed. She knew their story. She could see into their minds.

They said this place was transitional and they were to move on to a higher place. They told her they had a choice. We can be reborn, we will know our lives, the span of time and the lessons we must learn.

Ian continued: 'But when we are reborn into the new life, we will forget all that has been revealed to us and the lessons we have to learn from that life.'

Matthew was communicating again: 'But we have decided to move on mother, to a higher plane. We have chosen not to be reborn.'

'Can I come with you?' She saw the sadness and felt the pain.

'You have a learning path, Mother. It was only chance that brought you here today, when we were preparing to leave this plane.'

'What will happen to me? I just found you and now you are moving on.' She felt a terrible sadness but realised she could have missed them completely.

'You will leave here; you will learn and be helped and eventually given a choice as we were.' Matthew took her hand as he was leaving. 'Goodbye Mother,' and both boys gradually faded away.

She should have felt the pangs of loss again but she felt strong and alive. She knew her boys were in a better place.

She thought of Jack and the lunch and how he would feel when he found her dead in her favourite armchair and in a blink she was back and Jack had hold of her hands.

'Come on love, wake up, you need to change, its nearly time we were off. I thought you were coming to pick me up in your car.'

'Oh Jack, my love, I've been to heaven to see Matthew and Ian. I only just caught them; they were on their way to a higher plane.'

Jack laughed, 'You've been dreaming silly; come on get your coat on, we'll be late.'

How Did You Know?
MARY JEAN SINCLAIR

Half an hour before I need to go to Sunday school. I'm busy podding peas for dinner, my favourite job; popping the odd one into my mouth as I go along. They are delicious. Mam is putting the joint in the oven. My two brothers are out playing as usual.

'I have a surprise for you,' Mam says. 'We are having a baby next year'. Phew what a surprise. What an absolutely wonderful surprise. I throw my arms around Mam. She knows how well I look after my dolls and I love dressing them and swapping clothes around. A real life doll! I can't believe we will have a real baby, goodness. John was 10. Wonder what he will feel about no longer being the youngest. I skipped ecstatically all the way to St. Aidan's, wondering how, having promised Mam that I wouldn't tell everyone. I wanted to shout for joy and tell the world.

When I'd calmed down a bit, I started to wonder why Mam wanted a baby. She worked hard looking after us 3 and Dad and we never had any money. We didn't have a car and Mam used to take us everywhere on the bus since we became too big to fit on their bikes with them. We couldn't afford a bike each for us three. Didn't make sense to me; but then grownups often didn't.

Time dragged by so slowly. By Christmas, Mam was always tired and having to rest. She'd put on a lot of weight and I suppose the worry of having the baby was getting to her. I suppose she was old to be having a baby, she was nearly 40. I was having to do more and more about the house, but I didn't mind at all. I loved cooking and ironing and sweeping up. We didn't have a vacuum cleaner or a washing machine. Not many people did!

The baby, apparently was due in the middle of February and the Midwife kept coming round to check the house was suitable for a new baby…don't know what business it was of hers, but she was nice. Dad was going to have a trip off sea to look after us as we couldn't afford to have someone come in. That would be fun. Dad never had to do any housework or cook. I could do both, so we'd manage. Mrs. Scott was going to come in the day we got the baby. She was alright but could be a bit fussy. The boys didn't like her as she was always nagging them about getting dirty. They were boys for goodness sake. You expect boys to get dirty.

I have to confess that I was praying we would have a girl. I used to gaze at pretty dresses when I was out shopping and longed to be able to buy them. I was getting good at sewing with the Singer sewing machine so I would learn to make pretty dresses. Mam made all my clothes. I never once planned for a brother. Two of those were enough.

February the 18th I got up at 7:30 as usual. It was a Saturday, so no school. Mam was up already and groaning with tummy ache…something she'd eaten I supposed. She'd sent Bob round on his bike to fetch Mrs. Scott and then he had to go get the Midwife. Mam said the baby was coming today.

'How did you know?' I asked. She just smiled and groaned again. Seemed bad timing to me. Daddy wasn't due home for a couple of days and Mam wasn't feeling well with this tummy bug. I think she should have waited a few days when things had settled down and it was more convenient, but I kept quiet. She had enough to worry about.

But she was right. At 9 o'clock we were called into the front room to meet our new sister. The Midwife had put Mam into bed and she was looking very pale but holding a beautiful baby girl. My face wouldn't stop smiling. I gave my heart to this darling baby, and I never got it back. The Midwife kept saying Mam should go to the hospital. Something about losing too much blood. No idea what that was about but she wouldn't leave us. After the Midwife had bathed the baby, she gave her to me and said Mam had to go to sleep and we were not to worry her. I wasn't looking forward to changing nappies but Mam really was very tired so I had to do it, Mrs. Scott cooked us some dinner but it was horrible. Fortunately she was very happy to let me cook Sunday dinner whilst she looked after Mam and the baby.

Daddy came home a couple of days later. I expected him to be cross because Mam had got the baby early without him but he seemed delighted. He's lovely, is my dad. He never gets cross or moans about anything. I think he was nearly crying. He said a girl evened things out nicely and he had two girls now to sit on his knee. I knew I'd still be his favourite because he always sang 'I dream of Jeannie with the light brown hair' which he had written just for me.

Having a real living baby was tons more fun than playing with dolls. We all had a discussion about what to call her. Eventually we decided on Margaret Rose. We had to wait until Mam was better before we could take her to Church and get her Christened. Fortunately, we had got the pram bought before so I could take her out with me to do the shopping and to get some fresh air.

Mam was poorly for weeks. She had blood clots in both her legs so had to stay in bed and the Midwife came in every week to bandage them up with some horrible black smelly stuff. I soon learned to bathe Margaret and change her. I couldn't wait to get home from school to look after her. You could certainly say that baby changed my life. Wonder if that's why I became a Midwife when I grew up.

How To Make Finger Crisps
TRACY TODD

We were supposed to go on holiday two days ago, but didn't. You might think, 'Ah the bad weather, all that snow downed the plane,' and yes, that was a major factor, but not the whole story. You see, my crazy, single, husband decided he would warm us up with some homemade, finger crisps. 'Very sweet of him,' I hear you say, 'What are finger crisps?' Let me explain.

I was sitting quietly in the dining room. Okay, I was hiding in the dining room – not wanting to be involved. I thought, if I stuck my head behind a book, I might be left alone. My husband, mother and son were fussing around in the kitchen all trying to be cooks. It was supposed to be homemade chips – all fat and greasy to fill a cold tummy, but somehow it turned into homemade crisps.

Of course, to make crisps at home you need a food processor, or, at least you do if you're my husband. It's quite simple really. You push peeled potatoes into the slicer and it slices thin bits of potatoes ready to be deep fried. Or, if you are too lazy to slice the potatoes into smaller pieces that will go through the funnel of the protective cover, you take off the protective cover and, with your bare fingers, just push the potatoes onto the 'extremely' sharp , revolving blades, whilst telling your son and mother-in-law: 'This is not the way to do this. It's dangerous.'

THEN... low and behold, before you know it, you are making homemade finger crisps, as you slice the top of two fingers off and scream in agony as 'tomato ketchup' blood drips all over the place.

'What now?' I think from my peaceful hideaway, totally unaware of the growing panic and chaos in the kitchen. I wonder if I stay quiet, snuggle deeper under my blanket and cover my head with my book, I can, somehow, become invisible and avoid whatever is causing the screeches in the kitchen. But, it is not to be! My mother crashes into the room in utter terror.

'Tracy, come quick.... his fingers, blood. I feel faint… can't stand blood.'

My son charges in after her, tears in his eyes.

'Mummy, mummy.'

Normally, I would say my mother is a very capable person, but blood does something to her brain. Perhaps in a previous life, she was a vampire and knows if she sees blood, she will suck someone dry. Or perhaps it really stems from my older brother, aged six, crashing through a glass door and slicing his arm through to the bone.

I look at the panic stricken faces of my mother and son and think, I can:

a) Ignore them

b) Run away

c) Help

Sighing, I pull myself up off the comfortable sofa, and leaving behind the lives in my book, I walk to the kitchen amidst growing shrieks. My husband's holding his dripping hand over the sink; a tea cloth already red as he tries to stem the bleeding.

'Take Adam and go away!'

I order my blubbering mother and child. Relieved, they hide in the middle room as I call for a taxi to dash us to the emergency ward.

The plane managed to dodge the flakes and zoom away to warmer climes without us, whilst my husband stayed home, taking care of his finger crisps and nursing his cauterized blood vessels.

The Old Man
JEAN WILLETT

There's a tired old man at the back of the bus,
Along time ago he was just like us.
Busily going from place to place,
A paid up member of the human race.

One day he was called to fight a war,
Became disillusioned with what he saw.
The inhumanity of man to man,
Being told it was part of a bigger plan.

Then discharged with nerves all shattered
World in turmoil, a life in tatters.
Friends and family turned their backs
Love and support are all he lacks.

Where's our compassion? Where's our caring?
Kids nearby are laughing and jeering
Don't join in, just hold out your hand,
Remember he fought to save this land.

Let's not forget heroes, let's not forget war
Let's try to make sure he suffers no more.
Let's do our bit as he did for us
That sad old man at the back of the bus.

A Family Affair
GORDON WILSON

As you near the door of The Lord Raglan, catch the warm waft of malt and hops; hear the voice of Johnny Ray within; observe the figure of Paul Briggs urgently crossing Riby Square, nipping and tucking between fish wagons and coal trucks. His new white, silk-lined mackintosh is open, flapping cape-like as he strides toward the step. As he cuts in front of you with no word of 'excuse me', note the seriousness of his face, the intensity of his eye, the stone-like cast of his grimace. Follow him inside.

The shilling is slapped on the polished wooden bar. Curtly he orders 'half-shandy.' The barmaid receives no thanks on delivery. Bring your own drink to the table by the wall.

Paul's feet are tapping, counter to the rhythm of the Nat King Cole song.   His brown brogues, beneath fawn-coloured Oxford bags, rest alternately, left, then right, on the brass foot-rail that runs parallel with the curving bar. This pattern is interrupted by occasional bursts of soft stamping on the spot on the terra-cotta floor.

The hand that is whitened by its firm grip on the glass is smooth, unmarked by hard labour, unscarred by gutting knives or black frost, unlike those of most men in this bar. The hand that holds the cigarette moves more regularly than you might expect between ashtray and tight lips, and is often tapped, unnecessarily, above the floor.

Notice the rise and fall of this young man's shoulders. He is breathing heavily. An index finger wipes an eye. Is it a tear of sorrow, or a cigarette-smoke irritation? Despite frequent lifting to his mouth, the level of the beer in his glass barely falls.

Paul Briggs' eyes are fixed. He does not look at you. Nor does he observe the frail-looking man in the corner of the room. Nobody pays much attention to Hector Brumby, once promising fisherman, now regular drunk. Paul ignores the dart game at the far end of the bar and the domino and card schools on the window side of the pub.

Across the foggy room, around a circular table by the toilets, sit six people: three men, three women. They have, evidently been here some time. Two men have their backs turned. One woman's face cannot be seen. The other two have deep red painted lips, all three have beehive hair. One of them is laughing, loudly, showing tobacco-stained teeth and a white-coated tongue. Between them sits a man. He is dressed in the pleated-backed, powder blue suit that is the new fashion of the trawlerman ashore. The slowly drying stains on his trousers indicate the limited success of a recent trip. The broad white shirt collar overlaps the coat, revealing a hirsute chest beneath a clean-shaven neck and chin. He nuzzles the neck of the brunette, whose hooting delight and wide-eyed mock surprise suggest something secretly said. He lights three cigarettes, passing one to each of his female companions. It is upon this man that Paul's anguished eyes are keenly focused. The man does not register the attention that is upon him. Much of what he sees today will be blurred, for Albert Briggs is drunk and apparently destined to become more so. The brunette stands, lifting glass and cigarette, offering an accompaniment to the voice of Rosemary Clooney, which spills from the jukebox.

Not an hour before you first saw him, Paul had left the men's outfitters where he works and cycled home for lunch. He had left his bicycle by the back-gate, as usual, and, on entering the door, seen the long, thin, black sea-bag that marked his father's homecoming. Removing his coat, he had been surprised at the absence of the pungent odour of navy-rum that usually signalled Albert Briggs' presence. The radio was playing softly.

He had found his mother, Ellen, on the floor, beside the overturned coffee table with its Wild-West landscape under broken glass. He went to lift her. His first thought was that she was dead, then he saw her breasts rise beneath her torn blouse as he rolled her face aside. Ellen's left eye was closed and swollen. Her right cheek-bone was brightly red and her bottom lip broken and fat. She woke in his arms and sobbed. After carrying her to the settee he sat with her, silently, as she wept.

Never, before, had it come to this. All through his childhood there had been rows. Often, he had been woken in the night by his shouting or her screaming. She had been called things that Paul, at first, had not understood but later learnt the cruelty of. There had been times when he and Ellen had gone away, sometimes to Grandad's in Lowestoft, but they had always come back. Paul had wondered why but never asked. They had always made-up but never had Paul's veil of fear been pushed back fully. He had seldom known affection from the man. At night Paul had heard Albert complain about him to his mother. She had said that he was fussing unnecessarily, that not every boy was made in Albert Briggs' image.

Ellen's breathing calmed and she went to make tea, insisting she was all right. The radio played a Frankie Laine song. Paul followed, watching her, questioning.

'Yes, it was him,' she said sniffing, lifting a still trembling hand to draw deeply on the cigarette. 'He came in drunk, straight off the ship. He wanted to know why there was no breakfast waiting. He asked if I'd given it to my fancy-man.' She looked away here, to the window, then continued. 'He said he hoped I'd have the sheets washed before he came back at teatime. I said to him, 'Who do you think you are questioning my behaviour, you of all people?' The womanising whoremonger. 'You're welcome to walk out of that door and never return as soon as you like,' I told him. Then he turned and hit me. I was falling, then he grabbed me by the blouse and held me while he hit me again, two, three times, I can't remember how many. All the time he was telling me the house was in his name and I'd best not forget it. Then he left. I just wanted to die, Paul. I just laid down there and must have cried myself to sleep.' Paul had held her close, stroked her hair, guided her to the settee.

He had heard Albert question his mother's honour before but he'd always known the claims were made in drink and without foundation. She was a wonderful mother and, he often thought, a too tolerant and faithful wife. He had often thought she might be wise to find another man, dreamt of her remarrying. There had never been a doubt in his mind that they could adjust to life without Albert Briggs.

Paul dabbed Ellen's wounds with TCP. He'd brought her a cardigan when the shivering began and put her to bed with hot-water-bottle. He would leave her there before getting ready to go back to work.

He had never spoken against Albert before but could not hold his tongue this time. Even then, years of ingrained automatic respect and adherence to the Fifth Commandment, but mostly fear, tempered his response to the situation.

'I hope that none of his temper ever shows up in me,' he had said and, weeping, added, 'Why ever did you marry that brute, Mam?'

Ellen had held his head between her hands, kissed his nose, wiped tears away and told Paul things he had never known.

***

Watch Paul as he moves five long paces around the curving bar to stand in full view of the man and his friends. Albert looks up, stares, slowly focusing on the figure before him. Standing, slowly he bellows, 'Well look who's here. It's my little boy Paul. The scrawny little get!' Paul does not respond but continues to stare. 'What are you doing here, little Paul? This is a man's pub.'

'You're pissed.'

'And you're a puff! Do you all know that? My boy's a poncey puff. He's a member of the Church Fell-ow-ship Dra-ma-tic Soc-i-e-ty. An ac-tor. He wears make-up! Isn't that right, son, all powder and paint like a bloody tart!'

Dominoes and cards are downed. The dartsmen look on.

'You'd know more about tarts than I do,' Paul responds.

'Well, you little bastard!' the blond woman says, but Paul does not hear and continues in a trembling voice.

'Do you treat these women the way you treat my mother? Well, do you?'

'And do you know what he does for a living? He's a tailor. He measures inside legs. I'm going to buy him a sewing machine for Christmas.'

'When he takes you home, girls, does he bust your lip? Does he black your eyes? Does he bruise your cheek-bones? Does he...'

And what are you going to do about it? Stitch me up?' Albert has stepped around the table now to stand before Paul, looking down at his head. 'You little cissy wimp. You make a man ashamed to call you, son.'

Hear the hissed response as Paul's head tilts to look him in the eye. 'Thank Christ I'm no son of yours.' Albert's eyes widen and the snarling softens as he mentally adjusts, though his posture remains fixed as Paul says more. 'She was pregnant when she went to live with you. She said you were too stupid to work out the dates...too arrogant to imagine she might still have been sleeping with the man she left you for.'

Albert responds, through a slowly breaking crooked smile, 'Your mother's no more than a whore.'

Observe the pain distorting the young man's face. The twist of the mouth as the eyes fill with tears. The head bows and soft hair hangs loose. The right arm reaches behind to the bar for a glass that splinters as the twisting wrist strikes it on the bar. There is a blurring arc as it swings down, then up, and across Albert Brigg's throat. The blood floods his shirt front, sprays Paul's mackintosh, showers the bar-top, splashes, rattling on the tiled floor.

Albert falls. Women scream. A man rushes with a towel to stem the flow. Paul Briggs turns and walks briskly from the room.

Observe Hector Brumby, back bent, creeping around the bar to survey the scene.

Margaret
VALERIE WYNNE

'Sit here, Margaret.'

A woman guides me to a plump armchair. It looks comfy so I do as I am told. There are people all around me, sitting, just sitting; not talking, not smiling, just sitting. The sun is shining through the windows and the seat cushions feel nice and warm but something is wrong. I feel hot and tense, ready to spring into action. I don't know these people.

'AAAAAGH!' a long scream, like the screeching of a steam train's whistle echoes round the room. The woman jumps and spins round to look at me. Did I do that? Yes, I did!

'Help, help!'

'Margaret, would you like a cup of tea?'

A young girl has a trolley, with cups of tea and biscuits. I like biscuits. I take a packet of custard creams and a cup of tea. The cup is nice and warm in my hands and I hold it tight. There is something I am supposed to do, but I can't remember. I hold the cup carefully so that it doesn't spill and try to think.

'Don't forget to drink your tea, Margaret.'

That's it, drink up. I like tea and biscuits. Drink my tea, eat my biscuits. That's what I have to do. There is something more though. It's like running through treacle, getting my brain to work. It's all there, inside my head, but I can't push through the treacle to get to it. My memories are out of reach. I stretch back, trying, trying, but I can't quite make it. I am in here. I know I am. Let me out, let me out!

'Help, help!' There goes that shouting again.

'It's all right, Margaret. Let me take your cup for you.'

The cold mug of tea is placed on the table, next to the custard creams. I look around at the others, sitting. I can hear music playing but none of us are listening. We are sitting, just sitting.

There is a draught of cold air as the outside door is opened wide and a lady and her dog walk inside. I sit up straighter in my chair and look at it. It looks back at me and its tail starts to wag. The chunky yellow Labrador trots over to me along with its owner. I stroke her head and ears and I feel the weight of her leaning against my legs. Thump, thump, her tail beats a tattoo on the side of my chair. The treacle mush in my brain starts to thin and I begin to break free.

'Would you like to give Honey one of these treats, Margaret?'

I reach out for the bone shaped biscuit.

'My name is Maggie. I used to have a dog, you know, she was called Lucky. She was a mongrel, a Heinz 57 we used to say. Jim and I had her for 15 years. How old is Honey?'

'She is 2 years old, so I hope to have her for a long time

yet, then,' came the reply.

It was lovely to feel her, so soft, so alive beneath my hand. Her eyes looked full of warmth and trust.

'Good girl, good girl,' I murmured, 'How old is she?'

'She is 2 years old,' came the reply.

I looked around. Other hands were stretched out. Smiling faces called Honey's name.

She moved on around the group and I watched. I remembered Lucky and I remembered Jim too. How we had walked round the park holding hands. We would sit at one of the tables outside the café. I would have a cup of tea and Jim would have coffee. He used to tease me for dunking my custard creams in my tea, but I loved them sweet and soggy, and so did Lucky, when I shared, that is. I sat and remembered, a happy smile on my face as I ate my biscuits.

The lovely, chunky Labrador snuffled my fingers, looking for custard cream crumbs. I patted her head.

'Too late!' I said, 'What a lovely dog. What is her name? How old is she?'

Good Old Public Transport
GRAHAM ALBECK

Today I took a little ride on a local Stagecoach Bus
With Kids and Parents on there as well kicking up a fuss.
I took my turn in the queue and then I showed my pass
The driver said, 'Sit where you want mate cos, we only have
one class.'

Down the road for half a mile till we came to a red traffic light
Where the driver stopped real quick and gave us all a fright!
So off we went again with nerves all shook to hell
But within twenty seconds we stopped again 'cos someone had
rung the bell!

After half an hour or so I'd reached my destination
Where I'd arranged to meet a friend at the railway station.
On my return journey there was only the driver, a woman and
me
But I really can't complain, now that I can travel for free!

Play It For Gran
DAVID BROMLEY

As he sat on the number 10 bus going around Hyde Park Corner, Jonathan Scarne wondered whether this was some kind of bad joke his friends were playing on him. The phone call an hour earlier from his violin tutor at the Royal Academy of Music sounded genuine enough but it is not that hard to mimic someone's voice.

Jonathan had been in bed in a state half way between sleep and wakefulness when his mobile phone's ringtone, the opening bars of the 1812 overture, had brought him to full consciousness. It was his tutor from the Royal Academy, Steven Cotterill.

'Sorry to wake you, but there's a job if you want it, but it's for tonight,' said Steven. 'I hope you did not go too wild at the party last night,' he continued, 'because this could be your big chance.'

Suddenly, Jonathan was wide-awake and attentive. 'A job? What kind of job?'

'Its at the Hall. Old Solomon has gone down with food poisoning. He was due to perform Mozart's Violin Concerto No. 5, the same piece that you played at the graduation concert and Rollo who is conducting tonight was so impressed that he wants you to perform it in Solomon's place. So just nip along now, he's at the Hall and don't forget to take your violin. I must go I have a busy day, but cut along, time is short.'

It was only after Steven had ended the call that Jonathan began having doubts. It had only been a week since he had graduated from the Royal Academy. The Hall Steven had referred to was The Royal Albert Hall, Solomon was Solomon Gravitch, possibly the finest violin soloist of his day, Rollo was Sir Rollo Miles conductor of the Royal Philharmonic and the concert was The Last Night of the Proms.

Despite his doubts he could not ignore the summons, just in case. Jonathan showered quickly and dressed in jeans and a clean T-shirt and grabbing his violin case set off. The nearer his bus got to the concert hall the more convinced he became that he would discover it to be a wind up. Yet to his surprise when he arrived at the artist's entrance he was expected and the doorkeeper directed him to one of the main dressing rooms. After a few minutes Sir Rollo's PA came into the room and explained that the great man was rehearsing with one of the other soloists but would be ready for Jonathan in about an hour. In the meantime would he like something to drink, tea or coffee?

Even as he sat waiting to see the Maestro he still felt sure it was some kind of mistake and Sir Rollo had possibly got him mixed up with another violinist. He still did not believe it was happening but even so his whole body was shaking at the very thought of it.

It was nearly ninety minutes later when the P.A collected him and lead him on to the stage of the great building. The clear area in front of the stage where that evening the Promenaders would be standing, stamping and flag waving was empty except for some TV people setting up their equipment. The orchestra, all casually dressed, sat in their positions idly chatting to each other whilst Sir Rollo was studying a music score.

'Ah, Jonathan,' said Sir Rollo, shaking him by the hand, 'thanks for stepping into the breach.'

'Thank you, Sir Rollo, but please why me?'

'Three reasons really,' the Maestro answered, 'because of the timings for the television we have to keep the piece in the program, secondly there was no way we could get any of the big names in at such short notice but mainly because I heard you play the concerto at the college concert and was impressed.'

If he had been entirely truthful Sir Rollo might also have added that the publicity and interest to be gained from plucking a virtual unknown and placing him in front of a world audience would guarantee maximum media coverage.

They rehearsed the concerto twice, once for the benefit of the musicians and once for the television crew. After they had finished Sir Rollo congratulated him and introduced him to Martin Ryder, the leader and first violinist of the orchestra.

With a 'Well done, you'll be fine my boy' Sir Rollo swept

off the stage followed by his P.A.

'How do you feel about it?' Martin asked.

'To tell you the truth, I feel absolutely terrified. I still can't stop shaking. I really don't know if I can do it.'

'Of course you can, the rehearsal went well. You'll have no problems, the last night audiences come to enjoy themselves so everything will be fine.' Even these encouraging words did little to calm Jonathan down.

The afternoon was chaotic, firstly Jonathan had to go back on stage and rehearse his entrance and exit and possible encore for the benefit of the camera crews. Not that he believed that he would have to worry about an encore but it had to be rehearsed just in case. When the story had reached the press about an unknown performing at this prestigious event there had been a photo call and interviews. There was a television set in his dressing room and he had the strange experience of seeing himself on the BBC six o'clock news. Soon after that his Mother and Father who had also seen the News called him to wish him luck and to chide him for not letting them know about the performance himself.

As it got closer to the start of the concert Jonathan was getting close to panic.

He must have played or practiced the concerto a hundred times but just at that moment he could not remember a single note. Also he had never experienced stage fright before but now the thought of playing in front of five thousand concertgoers and millions of television viewers filled him with dread. The largest audience he had ever played to before was about two hundred and quite a few of them had been family or friends.

A couple of hours later, dressed in his normal concert rig of dinner jacket and black bow tie, a girl from the TV makeup department was dabbing and powdering his face, 'To prevent a glow from the TV lights,' she told him. His performance was due in the first half of the concert and soon after the makeup girl had left he could hear the audience arriving and various members of the orchestra tuning up.

On his way to the orchestra pit, Martin Ryder called in to wish him luck.

'How do you feel?' Martin asked

'If you want the truth, absolutely petrified.'

'Don't worry, it will be fine. I'll give you one tip that has stood me well, who do you like playing for best?'

'My Gran,' Jonathan replied without hesitation. 'She really likes it when I play for her and she even bought me my new violin when I won my place at the Academy.'

'Right,' said Martin, 'when you are out there forget all about the audience and the television, just think about your gran and how much you enjoy playing for her. I always think about my old teacher and it works for me every time.' And with that he left to join the rest of the orchestra.

Although it was warm back stage Jonathan felt decidedly cold. He took his violin and bow out of the case but they felt strange and awkward in his hands. He could not do this, he told himself and it was not fair of them to expect him to. He shouldn't be a soloist; he had only this week applied for a position as third violin in a provincial orchestra. After what he expected to be tonight's fiasco, he felt sure he would be lucky to even get that job.

The time had come. The message of doom came over the dressing room tanoy. Jonathan Scarne, 5 minutes please.' Well so be it, he had made up his mind what he would do, simply walk out onto the stage, apologise to the audience and walk off. That was definitely the best thing. As he made his way towards the stage he wished he were anywhere but there.

With his violin in one hand and the bow in the other Jonathan walked out on to the stage amidst thunderous applause and cheering from the Promanaders. Even the members of the orchestra were clapping him. He did not expect they would be so generous when he made his announcement. Sir Rollo leaned over from his dais and shook his hand. Then the leader Martin leaned forward and offered his hand and as they shook he mouthed the words to Jonathan, 'Play for your Gran.'

They exchanged a smile and Jonathan turned to the audience. This was going to be the moment he made his apology, but he couldn't. Slowly and automatically he placed the violin under his chin and raised his bow. Although there were five thousand people in front of him he suddenly felt he was in a cocoon of isolation and could only see one face in his mind.

That evening at The Royal Albert Hall a new star was born. It was a star destined to shine for a very long time. In the years that followed no matter how large the audience or big the occasion Sir Jonathan Scarne, the world famous violinist, always imagined he could see just one face smiling back at him.

Holy Island Arran
BRENDA COLE

Standing alone proud to the sea
The grey mist swirl invisibility
Isolation, yet all life, fresh winds biting
Rocks alighting
Gulls screeching, swooping down on thermal ranges
Cumulous clouds standing waiting

Piles of sea weed stinking rotting
Water's lap the shore's mocking
White horses ride the crested waves
coming to rest inside the caves

Shells from meals the birds have left
Whole carcasses of fish bereft
Driftwood caught in tangled weed
waiting waves to be freed

Limpets stick like hard cement
Curlews cry their wild lament
Perfumed air of salt sprayed dunes

Sand so soft as left marooned

Splashing spray falls so free
With an air of tranquillity
Through the clearing of the mist
Pools of sun kissed waters glisten
Algae softens craggy edges
Whispering voices through the reeds, listen
Mysterious communication feeds

On the horizon towards the shore
a rainbow glorious colours and more
Triumph outlined in majestic purple
Feeling overwhelmed with awe
Touch the nerve cells to the core.

The Masterpiece
JACQUELINE COLLINS

The three people in Freemans office were certain they would inherit portrait artist Jed Masterson's fortune. Masterson, had the ability to capture the very essence of a person. Once he recognised this in a subject, he had to paint them. Miss Pimlico's innocence, Frau Penge's passion, John Robert's pride

He had promised his fortune to each when he painted them, believing theirs the greatest portrait, he would ever paint.

Freeman announced Masterson left everything to 'Homer' his wolf hound, his latest subject, his greatest achievement. Homer padded out from under the desk, not sure why he was here at all.

Grown Children
DAVE EVARDSON

Onto the bus, out of the gate
Away from the factory & trading estate
Onto the trunk road, & into the town
Another day over, you're winding down

Face at the window, what can you see?
Everyone's going home just like me
End of this road here, lights are on red
Smile at a girl but she turns her head

On through the centre, slow as a snail
Usual snarl-up, planners prevail
Over the crossing, jammed at the square
Sprawled on an old bench, you meet his stare

Grimy the face, blank & hollow
The eyes go through you, try not to follow
Dark, the reflected remains of his past
He must have had one, it just didn't last

Yes, the face is familiar, you roll back the years

A child in the playground with first morning fears
Eyes locked for a second, you wanted to say ...
Then someone called out & you went back to play

Family tragedy? Loss of his wife?
What could have happened to cripple his life?
Hand on the bottle, up to the lips
Suckles the grown child with black fingertips

You wonder how old? Younger than me?
With a wash & a brush-up he'd pass for forty
He's looking around now, a questioning eye
Perplexed by a world that just passes him by

Then smiting the air, the whole street harassing
He's swearing at no-one & everyone passing
Embarrassing now, if his senses improve
And he catches your eye. Will this bus never move?

And it does with a jolt, & soon you're back home
With the kids & the paper, the evening to come
She asks what your day was like, tells you of hers
Then tea-time & TV & going upstairs

Just briefly you wonder where he'll spend the night
Who's taking his hand as he turns out the light?
You're only grown children whose lives nearly met
Pull up the bedclothes, best to forget

Now The Postman Smiles
RON GEDDES

He saw her in the queue, patiently waiting for stamps for her mail. With her elfin features, mane of brunette hair held in a ponytail and small smile, she lit up his life. Over the past few months he battled his shyness and knew her name was Jennifer. The first time she spoke his name 'Colin', his heart took a day to return from his mouth. Colin, a man in his late twenties, worked for Australian post, which required moving around the city relieving absent staff. He was immediately recognisable as he wore an old grey cardigan at work, mainly because all year around, the shops were kept at an even, cold seventeen degrees centigrade.

As the queue decreased, she came to his window.

'A dozen stamps please, Colin.'

'No problem, Jennifer.'

She paid the bill but seemed to be in no hurry to leave. There was no one waiting, so Colin ventured some conversation.

'So, is business good?'

'Yes, I co-ordinate things for Medicare when they look after people in their homes.'

'Is it interesting?'

'Sometimes, but satisfying. It's actually a lot of responsibility for someone not yet thirty. Oh. I forgot. One of the things we do is take care of old people's mail. There's a new lady in the program and she's asked for her post to be redirected to us.'

She handed over the instruction.

'You look after an awful lot of folks,' commented Colin.

'Yes, almost a thousand, all over the country.'

Jennifer was fast running out of small talk. She opted not to hold back or leave, but spat the words out like a chattering machine gun.

'Why don't you come down when you have a break and sample some of my tea?'

Colin blushed, but thinly smiled.

'That sounds good.'

Bringing de-lux biscuits, Colin took Jennifer up on her offer. Surprisingly, the get together sparkled as they began to get to know about the other. Jennifer lived at home with her strict parents and desperately wanted to leave. He lived in digs with some mates. Originally it was for a week or so but now, months were passed and the flat was no longer a stop gap; just a gap.

'It would be nice to have my own pad,' said Jennifer, 'but how do you afford it?'

'Yeah. Money's tight. I work as a stop gap PO clerk all

over Sydney relieving absent staff. It's better paying, but not a fortune.'

She said nothing. Colin continued.

'Do you often wonder why I don't openly smile at you, much as I would like to?'

She thought about it, realising unconsciously she only noticed it now, once he told her.

'I have a gum disease. It's plagued me ever since I was a teenager. Not very pleasant.'

'Show me,' she insisted.

He smiled broadly. It was the first time she had seen his teeth. He had precisely seven and was pleased when she did not flinch away.

'What's needed?' she asked.

'Extractions and either false teeth or implants and lots of money.'

'Go for the implants. After a car accident I had some replaced. See?'

He looked where she pointed.

'You'd never know.'

'Yes, God bless insurance.'

'Don't suppose you can organise a car accident on my behalf Jennifer?

'Not likely. I'd be unlucky to get one with no insurance.'

A glaze came over him as he went deep into himself.

'Colin, a penny for your thoughts?'

'Oh, sorry Jennifer,' he muttered abstractly. 'Perhaps motor vehicle is the wrong kind of insurance.'

During the next few weeks Colin formulated and began implementing his plan, ably abetted by Jennifer.

Knowing Post Office videos were only kept for seven days, it was to their advantage.

Jennifer would travel to a PO where Colin was working and post a letter from one of her care persons, after insuring the "valuable" inside, to another person in her system. Colin did the processing, a black biro slash over the bar code, ensuring it would join the hopelessly lost and unclaimed pile. When the parcel was a "no show/lost", a claim was lodged, usually processed by Colin. Both agreed the procedure was extremely efficient. With no repetition of sending office, poster or addressee, there was no connection, the Post Office even cashing their own compensation cheque.

It was six months later when Colin sat Jennifer down, his ten thousand-watt Pepsodent implants smile lighting up the cafe.

'Up for some more, or do we call it quits and skulk away Jenn?'

She nestled alongside him as lovers do with one another.

'Seeing the Post Office pays out millions a year in lost post, what about we keep going till we can afford that three-bedroom unit? And how about we take out and pay for some life insurance on some of my people, with me as the beneficiary naturally. It's more popular and common as a way of saying thank you than you think and doesn't erode or impact the estate's base assets.'

'You wouldn't believe it but the other day the doctor mixed up a patient and issued a death certificate for the wrong person. They deal with so many. And it's not an irregular occurrence, but happens more than you think.'

'Far out,' quipped Colin. 'Just make sure they contact you with the good news.'

Edgar Street (5th August 1914)
DENISE LIGHT

At Number 1 Edgar Street Nora Watson sat at her kitchen table staring into space. Cup of tea in hand she was trying to get her thoughts into some semblance of normality. Ever since the announcement last night she had been worrying. She had been stupid really to stay up to listen to the radio, to listen to the declaration of war. She would have found out this morning anyway. As it was she hadn't slept at all well which was not good for the day ahead.

Her husband Alf was on a seven day fishing trip in the North Sea. He was due back tomorrow. There had been a lot of talk recently that war was inevitable so Nora had been worried that Alf and his crew would be at risk out there. She told herself that Alf would be back safely tomorrow, after all hadn't he always survived some really bad storms. Alf was the skipper of the trawler Jupiter and if he could bring back a really good catch it would help them survive the next few weeks. She couldn't decide if the trawlers would still go out fishing or not now that they were at war.

Nora decided to walk to the market to see if there were any bargains. Her two boys were playing upstairs so she shouted them to get their shoes on. A few minutes later the three of them were walking down the street.

Meanwhile next door, at Number 3, Mabel Barker was in tears. Her husband George had gone off to work as usual but as he went out the door he had told her that he was going to enlist. He wasn't going to let those Germans win! He knew what Mabel's reaction would be so told her when she didn't have time to argue the point. What would she do if George went off to war? She only had him. How would she survive without a breadwinner in the house? Perhaps she would have to get a job.

It was a similar situation in some of the other houses in the street. Fathers, husbands and sons all keen to enlist and wives and mothers wanting to keep their families safe at home. At Number 10, Nellie Stephens sat down to breakfast with her 4 sons. She looked at them with pride. She had done a good job bringing them up after Jack had been killed. He had been washed overboard on a fishing trip up near Iceland. Foolish that skipper had been, taking them up there at that time of year when the storms were so bad. But Nellie had pulled herself together and concentrated on bringing up her boys the best she could. She was determined that they would all have decent jobs and that none of them would go to sea. But now Nellie could see that war was going to change all her plans. She wasn't stupid, she knew that the army would take her boys. At 19 and 17 Clive and Alan were just the right age. At least the two younger boys, Herbert age 15, and John 13, would be all right.

Nellie spoke directly to Clive. 'Now I expect you will want to go and enlist in the army'.

Clive nodded.

'Son, I want you to think carefully about this. A lot of young men your age are going to be doing the same. And what will happen to them. They will be given a uniform and a gun and expected to shoot the enemy. Could you do that?'

Clive thought for a moment, and then said: 'I think I could. Certainly if it was a case of kill or be killed.'

'Well I have a better idea. Why not look at going in a supporting role. I am sure they will need men to do stuff other than fight. I think you should try and find out what you could do. Perhaps you could use your expertise with engines to look after vehicles. And you, Alan, could do the same.'

The two boys looked at each other. Their mother was usually right. Even when they disagreed with her, which they had done often enough, it usually ended up with Nellie being right.

'Don't go rushing into things, that's all I'm saying,' said Nellie. 'Now you better get a move on and get off to work.'

At one of the houses, however, things were a bit different. Bill and Annie Deacon and their son Leonard lived at Number 11. Bill was a stern father and Leonard, as a result, was quite a meek young man. Unassuming in his ways, he tried to stay out of his father's notice as much as possible. When he left school he had gone to work in Gilbert Jones & Sons Solicitors as a junior clerk. Always conscientious about his work he had shown himself to be an asset to the firm and had been promoted to be Mr Arthur Jones' clerk. Leonard's mother was inordinately proud of her son.

At breakfast in the Deacon household Bill put down the newspaper and said to his son, 'I expect you will be enlisting in the army. I would suggest that you go for one of the best, go for the Kings Own Yorkshire Light Infantry'.

Bill's suggestions were never really suggestions. They were orders and none of his family were used to doing anything but obey. But this time he would get a shock, one he was certainly not ready for.

'No,' said Leonard. 'I'm not going to go in the army.'

'What? Oh, you're going to join the navy then. You have no experience of the sea, you'll be better off in the army'

'No father, I'm not going to fight.'

'Not going to fight! A son of mine being a coward!'

'I'm not a coward. In fact I think I'm being brave saying that I object to going to war.'

'Go to your room!'

'No father, I have to go to work. I'm not a child to be ordered about by you.'

And Leonard got up from the table, gave his mother a peck on the cheek, picked up his briefcase and was out the door before his father could manage to do anything.

'Well you'll be no son of mine if that's your attitude.'

'Oh Bill,' Annie cried

'Be quiet woman, and stop that snivelling!'

At Number 6 Millie Smith was still in bed. Not for her the daily rush to get going in the morning .She liked to have a much more languid start to the day. Still, she supposed she should get up. It had been Fred's turn last night and before going to bed they had listened to the declaration of war. Fred had been quite grave about the news.

'I may not be able to keep coming,' he told her.

'You mean because of the war?'

'Yes, I might have to go and fight. Don't want to, of course. I'd much rather stay with you'

He pulled her close and kissed Millie. She quite liked Fred but as with some of her other men, he liked her more than she liked him.

Millie opened the drawer in her bedside cabinet and added her earnings to the pile already there. She was beginning to get quite a decent amount. It certainly helped her keep the wolf from the door and eventually she hoped to move away, to somewhere she could earn big money.

She idly wondered if the war would make a difference to her. Of course, it wouldn't. There would always be men to pay her for what they wanted.

Later that morning Nora Watson was on her way home from the market. Her shopping bag was nearly empty and she looked worried. When she got to number 17 she stopped to talk to Jim Fielding who was doing some weeding.

'Now then Nora, how are you? Morning young Frank and you young Edwin.'

'Hello Mr Fielding,' chorused the boys.

'Hello Jim,' said Nora. 'I'm really worried. I've just been down the market and everything's got so expensive. I only managed to get a small piece of meat for the three of us. I do hope Alf has a good trip because I don't know what we'll be able to buy if things are as dear as this all the time.'

'Oh, that's not good news,' said Jim. 'Looks like I'll have to dig up my flowerbed. Think I might see about growing a few more vegetables. And you should do the same my dear, get those two scallywags to dig the garden for you.'

Nora said goodbye to Jim and with her two boys walked the rest of the way to her house. She was already starting to feel a bit more positive. The war wasn't going to be too bad. They would find a way to survive, her and her boys and hopefully Alf as well, She would start on the garden this afternoon!

Down And Out!
CHRISTINE McCRAE

London is the pits!

I wake about 8am, head heavy and thumping with pain. Body aching all over. Hands and feet numb with cold. Lice are making me scratch incessantly. I can feel the icy cold pavement through my sleeping bag as I lie there, a pathetic bundle of a man.

This is the West End and the rush to work has begun. A worker gives me a sly kick as he rushes past, and a wave of shame and hopelessness passes through me. I pull the sleeping bag over my face. This is all too much. Sleeping here on the pavement is truly degrading.

It's been a year now, same old story, lost job, lost home, lost partner, no money, no support, then on the street. Numbed the pain with alcohol, then tried a few drugs. Shortcut to a living hell.

Most days I pass my time begging. I try to sleep but mostly the enemy won't let me. They harass me and call me names like 'Scrounger' or 'Scumbag,' or worse. They're right I suppose. A lot of my time is spent stealing stuff in shops. Usually I manage to sell it on. I need the cash to survive, to get my drink and drugs to numb the pain.

Today I'll get some breakfast at my nearest charity shelter. Can usually get a wash there too. Later in the day there's the soup kitchen and whatever else is going. Always a lot of people hanging around. We catch up with a bit of gossip.

'Jack's out of prison tomorrow.'

'Smithy's been caught with his pockets full of swag in some shop.'

'Police had to break up a fight.'

And so it rolls on. The sad drama of the homeless.

If I'm still hungry I have a good old rifle through rubbish bins. Behind McDonalds you sometimes find a bit of burger or half eaten fruit. I also scout around the bins at the back of hotels. You can get rich pickings there if no one spots you.

There are some scary nutters on the street. They would steal the clothes off your back and the shoes off your feet. I wish I could sleep with one eye open!

You know it should never have been like this. Believe me when you get really down it can seem impossible to get up again. All your demons at once. Mental strength is what I need and I haven't got it. One day I will get the help I need.

Thought I'd enjoy a bit of luxury recently. Slept in the basement of a squat. Old Jim was there. He's been on the streets as long as he can remember. His teeth are a sight to behold. I said: 'Jim, you are a dentist's nightmare.'

He said: 'Well at least I don't need a toothbrush. Not worth it for two teeth!'

Jan was already there when we rolled up. He's looking pretty rough these days. He was out of it on something and lay curled up on some rags.

'Want a drink of water, mate?' I said.

There was a grunt and he curled up tighter on his bed.

Someone was shouting upstairs. Throwing things and cursing. Sounds like pots crashing. Hope they won't disturb we three homeless.

During the night there was a lot of blowing and moaning from Jan. 'Are you ok, Jan?' I whispered, but he had very little English and found it hard to communicate. Jim was snoring like a porker whichever position he was in. I managed to sleep for an hour or two by shoving tissue in my ears. Mind you I might snore myself!

Next day when I woke I went over to Jan. He'd had a rough night poor thing. I offered him some water but he was still. Too still. He was gone! Departed! Caput!

'Jim I think we'd better get out of here. Jan's snuffed it!'

'Oh, no,' said Jim.' We have to call an ambulance. Can't leave poor Jan on the floor. We haven't done anything. It's not our fault. It'll look suspicious if we just clear off.'

Another squatter was sitting at the door on the step. He was a skinny Rastafarian with his dreadlocks stuffed under a woolly hat. He was drawing heavily on a cigarette stub.

'Have you got a phone?' asked Billy.

'Here mate,' he said passing his phone.

Jim made the call and shortly after there was an ambulance with us. The paramedics quickly checked Jan. They could see that this was probably a natural death but we would have to be questioned by the police.

We trudged back to the West End, heavy of heart. We had just lost one of our mates on the floor of a filthy squat. We didn't know what to do next and some of the others were asking if anyone had seen Jan. Billy said he'd been unwell lately with chest pains and exhaustion. The writing had been on the wall so to speak.

Later that day the cops were there. They know us quite well. I've been inside a few times so I'm not a clean sheet! We had a bit of a grilling, but they said that Jan had probably died of natural causes. A post mortem would establish what had happened. Jim and I knew we had nothing to do with it.

A bit of a shocker though all the same and its put me off using that flee pit of a squat. We're back on the street tonight, safe or not!

A Day In The Life Of A Batlharos Doctor's Wife (And Some Meditations On It)
PAULINE MURDOCH

I live at the Doctor's place,
It's really rather jolly.
There's lots of children all about,
Especially now we've Johnny.

It's early rise at six o'clock
(the weather's getting chilly)
And off to Church for Mass we trot.
('Don't waken little Willy').

Next week we'll get a lie in bed
As Father's on the District.
But hurry now, the bell has gone,
And if we don't, we'll miss it.

The tune's too high, the words don't fit,
The incense makes me sneeze,
I do my best to meditate,
But Oh, my aching knees!

Then home we rush to dress the kids
And make a cup of tea.
There's someone knocking on the door –
It must be Mrs. P.

The baby cries, the phone rings loud.
Three times before I reach it;
The bacons burning in the pan,
And Susie's lost her breeches.

I haven't done the shopping list,
The Sandwiches aren't ready –
The Doctor's off to clinic now,
And Janet's lost her teddy.

The day goes on, the rush gets worse –
It's time for us to eat.
But goodness me – what has gone wrong –
They haven't sent the meat!

'No, Doctor's out.' 'What time he'll come?'
'I really couldn't say,
The road is rough, the clinic long,
Sometimes they lose the way.'

The goats got in again today,

And nibbled at the washing.
The mud the children get on them
Is really rather shocking.

It's time to feed the cat and dog,
The milk comes in a pail.
We put the kettle on for baths,
And baby starts to wail.

The children fed and tucked in bed,
It's time to think of supper.
It's then I find the fish hasn't come –
At least there's bread and butter.

'Yes dear, the supper's almost done –
You've got to ring the Sister –
Two patients waiting there since one,
And don't forget your lecture.'

The people in the nearest town
Who've seen us three times only,
Just knit their brows and shake their heads –
'You must be, oh so lonely!'

Near Kuruman, Northern Cape, R.S.A. (December 1963)

A Dogie Story
MARY SIMPSON

'Jasper. Jas-per.' Charlie braced himself as Jasper came charging down the garden path, his tail moving so fast, like a windscreen wiper in a downpour.

'Come on boy, paper round.' Jasper wagged faster as Charlie slipped the harness, lifting first his left paw and then his right, clipped it round his body – and fussed him as he fastened it.

Jasper was a twelfth birthday present. They were inseparable. Jasper accompanied Charlie on his paper round.

Charlie's mum watched out of the window as her boy and his dog went down the drive; she felt much happier about Charlie's paper round now that he had Jasper to look after him.

Charlie, tall for his fourteen years, with blond hair, fair skin and a happy disposition was shy, but Jasper helped him out with this. Lots of people stopped him.

'What kind of dog is that?'

'It's an Airedale,' he would reply.

'And how old is he?'

'He's four.'

'Where did you get him? You don't see many like that

these days.'

'We got him from an Airedale distress kennel.'

'He's certainly used to you.' And Charlie would smile, forgetting his shyness.

Charlie wanted to be home early; he'd got French and German homework and his mother's friend was calling to tutor him on his spoken German.

He tied Jasper outside the shop while he collected his papers.

When he came out, Jasper had a crowd of paper boys making a fuss of him.

'He's a great dog Charlie, wish he was mine.'

'You should ask your mum to get you one for your birthday, Jake.'

'Nah, they don't like dogs, my Mum and Dad.'

Charlie undid Jasper and hugged him. Jake gave Jasper another pat.

'You can always come round, Jake, on a Saturday or a Sunday.'

'That'll be great, thanks,' Jake responded.

Charlie delivered his last paper. His mobile rang – it was a text from his mother. 'Charlie, cum hm as soon as u can. Mr. Smith is cmg early and has only got a hr. x mum.'

Charlie texted back, 'Ok wil take sh.cut x pl.fields. xch.'

'Come on Jasper.'

Half way across the field, Charlie noticed three big lads

on the swings in the children's play area pushing the seats hard and watching them crash and bounce against the frames. They spotted Charlie and started across the field, making straight for him.

Charlie quickened his pace, he wasn't a coward but he avoided trouble when he saw it coming.

'Hey you, don't run off. Let's look at your dog. Is he any good at scrapping?'

Charlie used a bit of psychology, 'This breed fight to the death!'

'Stop then, let's look.' Charlie stopped. The eldest looking boy, a strapping lad, with a short haircut and an ear-ring moved to take the lead off Charlie. Quick as a flash Jasper had hold of the boy's arm making a fierce growling sound.

The boy jumped back with a start. 'Get that excuse for a dog off me!' Jasper hung on.

'Heel Jasper.' Charlie shouted and, straight away Jasper was back at his side.

'You'll be sorry for that!' he shouted as he raised his leg and gave Jasper a viscous kick in the stomach. Jasper yelped but got hold of the lad's trousers and shook; he lost his balance and ended up on the grass.

'Come on Jasper, let's go,' Charlie cried as he yanked his lead. They ran as fast as they could. Charlie turned round and saw the two younger boys helping the big brute onto his feet. Charlie and Jasper kept running.

'What on earth's the matter?' Charlie's mother cried as Charlie and Jasper dashed into the kitchen.

Catching his breath, Charlie explained what had happened.

'Did Jasper hurt the boy?'

'No Mum, he just got hold of his arm when he tried to take the lead and when the boy kicked him he got hold of his trousers and shook them and the boy fell over. He wasn't hurt at all.'

Mrs. Appleby took off Jasper's harness and looked at his stomach. When she touched the spot where the boy's boot connected, Jasper whimpered.

'There, there boy, I won't hurt you but we'll let the vet see this.'

'Mr. Smith isn't here yet Charlie, I think I'll put him off for tonight.'

When they got back from the vet, who said Jasper hadn't suffered any internal injury, Mrs. Appleby told Charlie she would be going to school to see the headmaster about the boys.

'They weren't from our school Mum; they didn't have uniforms and I didn't recognise them.'

'No more short cuts then Charlie, they seem like real ruffians.'

Two weeks later, Charlie had forgotten about the incident on the playing fields. He was collecting his papers in the back of the shop.

'Can you do an extra half round Charlie? '

'Yes Mr. Prentice.'

'John Norris is sick, if you do half, I'll get Ellis to do the other half, then you wont be home too late.'

Charlie finished his round and back at the shop to get the half round he was about to tie Jasper to the rail when he noticed Buster Howell, his mate and a dog – Jake had told him it was Buster Howell when Charlie had mentioned the confrontation on the playing field. Buster pulled his dog and shouted at him; he didn't even see Charlie and Jasper.

Wonder where he's going, his dog doesn't look very happy.

Charlie soon finished his half round and set off across the playing field, when he remembered his mother's 'keep away from short cuts Charlie.' Too late now; he was half way home anyway.

Then he saw Buster, his mate and his dog.

Crickey, I'll have to bluff it out.

'Hi Buster, nice dog.'

Buster scowled, 'A lot better than your wimp.'

'He could be a killer,' Charlie laughed, trying to be confident.

'Well let him try this then,' and he quickly unclipped his dog's lead. 'Get him Killer!'

Before he could get out of the way, Killer jumped on Jasper's back, digging his teeth into his neck.

'Get him off my dog Buster,' cried Charlie, moving in and

pulling hard on Killer's collar.

Killer turned, twisted his head round and sunk his teeth into Charlie's wrist and hung on. The blood started to spurt out of Charlie's veins as he screamed in pain, 'Get him off Buster.'

Buster's face paled as he pulled his dog away. Charlie yelled again as the dog's teeth dragged against his skin. As he fainted away, he saw Buster, his mate and Killer running away.

Jasper stood over Charlie, whimpered and licked his face, but to no avail, Charlie was out cold!

Mrs. Appleby heard scratching and barking at the door.

'Jasper, what's happened?' She saw the blood at the back of his neck, but before she could do anything, Jasper ran down the drive and stood, barking.

'What is it Jasper, where's Charlie?'

Jasper ran back up the drive and took Mrs. Appleby's skirt in his jaws and pulled.

'Paul,' she shouted, 'come quick, something has happened to Charlie.'

Mr. Appleby came out of the kitchen door.

'Come on Paul, Jasper will show us. Get your mobile; I don't know what's happened.' Jasper barked and pulled.

They followed him out of the drive, into the street and across the playing fields where Charlie lay, still unconscious.

'Look at his wrist Paul, it's been savaged.'

Paul was already on his mobile calling for an ambulance. Mrs. Appleby slipped out of her white cotton underskirt and bound Charlie's wrist tightly.

'Charlie,' Mrs. Appleby cried, holding him to her, 'I told you not to come this way.'

'We better get to the road,' Paul said as he lifted Charlie and put him over his shoulder.

'Give me your mobile Paul; I'll phone the police, it looks as if that bully has got himself a dangerous dog.'

The ambulance, and the medics, carrying a stretcher, were at the edge of the field and ran to meet them.

'We'll take him now sir.'

Mrs. Appleby gulped, trying to be brave.

'I'll go with him Paul, I think Jasper needs the vet.'

Paul looked at Jasper, lagging behind, the blood dripping from his wound.

'Come on, you clever boy, we'll get you looked at.'

Later that evening, everyone was at home. The police had apprehended Buster and Killer was in kennels until they decided whether the dog was dangerous or just unlucky having Buster as his owner.

Jasper had needed twelve stitches in his wound and Charlie needed twenty stitches in his wrist and arm.

Charlie explained what happened on the green to his mum, dad and the policeman.

'That's a very special dog you've got there Charlie,' the policeman said and patted Jasper gently on the top of his head.

Charlie put his good arm round Jasper and hugged him, 'Very, very special,' he replied.

What To Wear
JEAN WILLETT

Size eighteen bum, size sixteen trousers
Size twenty boobs, size eighteen blouses
I've done it again
I've put on weight
The weddings on Saturday
Can't diet, too late
Scour the shops for a suitable tent
From shop to shop
Energy spent
What's that in the distance?
A shop I've not tried
As I enter the door my joy I can't hide
The hangers all hold clothes suited to me
It's hard to decide which one of three
I finally choose an outfit in green
Wearing this I'll be proud to be seen
This shop's a godsend to the chunky fraternity
Who cares if it's called 'From here to maternity'?

Changes
VALERIE WYNNE

Tim stretched out on the sofa and had another drink of beer.

'Pizza, beer and Saturday T.V. Another perfect night.'

Carolyn cuddled up next to him but wasn't quite as quick to agree as she normally was. Saturday night in had lost a bit of its appeal.

'A Saturday night out once in a while wouldn't break the bank.'

She felt a bit guilty for having rebellious thoughts but once it was 'out there' this dissatisfaction started to spread. On Sunday they got up early and had a bike ride around the common before Tim got out his list of jobs and she put the Sunday roast on and prepped all the veggies. Whilst peeling and chopping, her mind wandered and she began to analyse their relationship. The kitchen must have been full of little thought bubbles bobbing around, as yet separate, not blending together.

If Tim noticed that she was a bit distracted during lunch, he didn't show it, in fact he was full of all his achievements, having mended the strimmer and found the reason why the back patio was full of moss.

'I spotted a blackbird tipping it all out of the gutter. I'll get up on the ladders later and set about giving them a good clean before we end up with damp patches.'

Tim was proud of the home they had saved so hard for and renovated together. He looked forward to the weekends when he could get to grips with all the little niggles that develop during the week. He was in his element changing washers, oiling hinges and mending wobbly chairs. He was calm and methodical and nothing on his list of jobs was put off or ignored.

She decided to tell her concerns to her friend Sue next time they met.

'Its not like I am unhappy, Sue. It's just that I feel like life has become very predictable. We have got into a bit of a rut.'

'If you feel like that, Lyn, then you need to spice things up a bit. Nothing too drastic,' she added, noticing the look of horror on Sue's face. 'I don't mean swinging from the chandeliers and wearing saucy underwear!'

'Thank goodness, I love my Bridget Jones specials,' laughed Carolyn.

They met regularly at the Singing Kettle in town and there was a pause as they both piled cream and jam on their scones…a tricky job which requires full concentration.

'Seriously though, if you want things to change, you are going to have to do something about it. You owe it to yourself and to Tim. I'm sure he loves you, its just that he likes his routines.' She took a deep breath, and added, 'and maybe you have got a bit boring too, Lyn. Use your imagination, ditch the big pants and get some nice, tasteful underwear. Decide what you want and let him know!'

Sue let the subject drop, they had been friends for ever and she had seen this conversation coming for ages but hoped that she hadn't been too blunt.

Truth be told, Carolyn was a bit hurt at first, but on reflection she had to admit that Sue was right. It wasn't just Tim's fault. He wasn't a mind reader, and maybe he fancied a bit of a change too.

Carolyn wasn't usually one to act impulsively, but later that day, she spotted Tim's list lying on the kitchen table after he had just emptied the toaster and without a second thought she added, buy Lyn some flowers, at the top of the list.

The next day, there was a lovely bunch of daffodils in pride of place on the kitchen table.

'I'd forgotten how much you love daffs,' Tim mumbled between kisses.

On Friday, Carolyn again spotted Tim's list lying next to her handbag on the coffee table.

Book Ristorante Italiano for Saturday night, she scribbled quickly.

Carolyn was late when she arrived at the Singing Kettle later that week.

'You look happy! In fact, you are positively glowing,' Sue

exclaimed as her friend plonked herself down.

'You bet I am! Tim gave me flowers in the week and we had a smooch in the kitchen, then on Saturday night, he took me out for a fantastic meal.'

Carolyn went on to explain her new strategy of adding to Tim's list of jobs.

'Wow, what a change, no wonder you look so happy, there is definitely a twinkle in your eye.'

'Oh, that's not from the flowers or the meal out,' Lyn laughed, 'but I'm not telling you what else I added to Tim's list.'

Skype
JOAN BARKER

It arrived in a box twelve inches square,
said on the label, 'Fragile. With care.'
My Christmas present from husband Bill'
he said, 'Come on, open it. If you don't I will.'

Wrappings off, revealed to my eyes,
a thingy, a whatsit, a definite surprise.
A Mecano gadget, a kind of robot,
to do all those jobs that I'd rather not.

Several neighbours have a Skype that lives in,
made at the same factory, from the same tin.
I input his programme to suit our life style
then watched my dinky domestic projectile.

Skype's morning routine is simple and sound,
to make the beds and tidy all round.
Clean the bathroom and kitchen sink.
Efficient and fast, all done in a blink.

An evening out dressed in our best,

leaving Skype in charge, a kind of test.
Programmed to ring us if need arose,
he sat on his dock, impatiently tapping his toes.

Answering my mobile to a policeman's voice,
'Madame come home, no, you've no choice'.
There's a serious incident at No 72,
a breach of the peace and it involves you.'

Skype the tyke invited his pals' round,
with lights all ablaze and riotous sound.
House cordoned off by armed response lot
they think it's a bomb scare, a terrorist squat.

'The house is surrounded Ma'am, aliens sighted.
Fears of an explosive device being ignited.
Too dangerous for you in there, too hectic.
What's that you say, it's your mechanical domestic?

They'd been in the cupboard the booze was in
and downed the lot, whisky, brandy and gin.
They were having a party, a Mecano ball
Identical robots sprawled out wall to wall.

Anybody want a robot, hardly used?
Been well maintained and never abused.
Will do all the jobs, whatever you choose.
Only remember-----to lock up your booze.

Fully Automated
JACQUELINE COLLINS

'Sid, what happened?'

'It's them new toilets Nurse. As I got off the loo it flushed. I spun around and looked down for the handle, there wasn't one. It flushed again, right in my face. Blinded, I felt my way along the wall. As I passed the drier, a blast of air took my breath away. I steadied myself at the sink, the taps sprayed all down me front. Exhausted, I sat on the bidet, it did an impression of the trevie fountain. I never touched a thing.'

Two am, cosy in bed, cocoa in hand, Sid, giggled. Bless him.

Sabrina
JEAN WILLETT

She'd been dozing and woke stretching her slender body languorously like a tiger resting in the jungle. She'd always been a beauty, the prettiest in a family of six girls. Her husband Si told her he'd got the pick of the bunch when he married her and she felt just as lucky to have won the heart of such a handsome man. Si worked as an airline pilot so she spent a lot of time alone, but when he returned home he spoiled her rotten.

As she rose from her comfy chair she glanced out of the window and almost jumped out of her skin. It was that woman again, staring at her through the glass. She was a scary sight with wild staring eyes and long matted hair. She almost looked like a scarecrow. It wasn't the first time she'd seen this strange apparition, she seemed to follow her around, making Sabrina quite nervous. She'd told Si about her but he said she must be imagining it. He told her to ignore it but she couldn't, she was scared, especially when she was alone.

Sabrina quickly pulled the curtains and went into the kitchen to close the blinds. She screamed as she saw the woman again staring at her through the back kitchen windows. Unable to rest Sabrina decided to take one of the pills prescribed for her anxiety. Switching the television on she tried to calm her fears but found it hard to concentrate on the drama being played out on screen. Maybe a drink would help, she thought, but soon one drink became many and an hour later she was snoring like a pig.

The sun shining brightly through the curtains woke her up; she'd slept all night on the sofa and was still in yesterday's clothes. Putting the kettle on Sabrina found she had no milk and deciding no one would notice her unkempt appearance she set off for the nearby supermarket. While she was there she picked up a couple of bottles of wine and a packet of cigarettes then she made her way to the fridge.

Suddenly she glanced sideways and there staring at her was the crazy woman again. Letting out a terrifying scream she dropped her shopping. Staff and customers alike ran to see what was wrong and to help her. She was kneeling on broken glass and howling like a wolf. All attempts to assist were rebuffed and she soon became aggressive. An ambulance was called and with kind words and gentle persuasion the paramedics managed to calm her down and dress her wounds.

The doctor who examined her at hospital was very gentle and tried to tell her that the woman she was seeing was an hallucination. At that she became aggressive once more. She stood up and pointed to the glass in the corridor door. Like a bat out of hell she ran to the door shouting 'There she is. I told you she was real. Well I'm going to put a stop to all this for once.'

There was an almighty crash as she smashed into the window showering herself with glass. Sabrina was immediately injected with Valium and the next she knew was waking up in a psychiatric ward. Two nurses were at the foot of her bed and she heard them talking.

'Poor woman,' said one; 'she was such a beauty up until a couple of years ago when her husband left her for one of his cabin crew. She can't seem to realise that the woman she's so afraid of is herself reflected in glass.'

The Lost Souls
MIKE COLLINS

Grimsby the Klondike of fishing after the trains came.

Young lads, lost souls, a burden of the parish.
Trawled up by the greedy, landed at the docks to exploit.

Promised, the silver darlings of the sea, plundered, by the sharks of the land.
Floundering on the decks in a storm, like the spoils of the net.

Owners smacking, skippers booting, mates belting, crews handling.
Being baited as cruel sports, like a fish on a line.

Run away from the boat. Sent back by the judge. Caste over with the buoys.
Died like the rest of the catch, gutted and battered.

Lost at sea, presumed drowned.

Funded by the National Lottery Community Fund, the Lincolnshire Writers project aims to establish and support new writing groups in the county, bringing together both experienced and new writers to share their love of writing

The support, provided by Hammond House, includes help with venue costs, creative writing workshops by qualified professionals and publication of the work produced by members.

If you are interested in leading or joining a group, you can find out more information and details of current groups at:

www.lincolnshirewriters.com

Promoting creative activities and supporting
talented people in pursuit of cultural development in
the community.

Other Publications:

Conflict: Award Winning Stories
Shakespeare in Debt
Eternal: Award Winning Stories
Eternal: Award Winning Poetry
Tales from the Walled Garden
Precious: Award Winning Stories
Precious: Award Winning Poetry
Who's Afraid of the Dark? Not Me!
Cows In Trees
The Dog with the Head Transplant

Available from most high street
and online booksellers and from:

www.hammondhousepublishing.com

International Writing Competition
Sponsored by the University Centre Grimsby.
Short stories, poetry, screenplay and theatre scripts
Find out more and enter on:
www.hammondhousepublishing.com

Lincolnshire Writers
Establishing and supporting for local writer's groups.
www.lincolnshirewriters.com

TV Channels
Cultural and community programmes showcasing
arts, literature, music and theatre
www.billboardtv.uk

Documentaries
Inspirational stories about people and organisations.
www.hammondhouseproductions.com

www.hammondhousepublishing.com